'It's not th[e]... B49 072 132 7 ...king you

Natalie Rivers grew up in the Sussex countryside. As a child she always loved to lose herself in a good book, or in games that gave free rein to her imagination. She went to Sheffield University, where she met her husband in the first week of term. It was love at first sight and they have been together ever since, moving to London after graduating, getting married and having two wonderful children.

After university Natalie worked in a lab at a medical research charity, and later retrained to be a primary school teacher. Now she is lucky enough to be able to combine her two favourite occupations—being a full-time mum and writing passionate romances.

CLAIMED FOR THE ITALIAN'S REVENGE

BY
NATALIE RIVERS

MILLS & BOON®
Pure reading pleasure™

First published in Great Britain 2008
Harlequin Mills & Boon Limited,
Eton House, 18-24 Paradise Road, Richmond, Surrey TW9 1SR

© Natalie Rivers 2008

ISBN: 978 0 263 86487 8

Set in Times Roman 10½ on 12¾ pt
01-1208-50174

Printed and bound in Spain
by Litografia Rosés, S.A., Barcelona

CLAIMED FOR THE ITALIAN'S REVENGE

For my friend, Rosemary

PROLOGUE

MARCO DE LUCA stood at the open window of the cottage, looking out into the clear, calm night. A full moon hung in the black sky and the sea stretched away into the darkness, lit only by the occasional silvery ripple of reflected moonlight.

For too many years he'd lived and worked in big cities, where the night sky was a hazy amber glow and the stars were virtually invisible. He'd driven himself so hard, building his business from scratch into the global enterprise that it was today, that he'd almost forgotten what it was like to slow down for a moment, to celebrate what he had achieved, or to appreciate the simple pleasures in his life.

There were no street-lamps here on this remote stretch of the Welsh coastline, filling the sky with their artificial light. And around the rugged bay where the cottage was nestled there were no other houses in sight.

It felt good to gaze out at the unblemished beauty of twinkling starlight in the inky black heavens, and at that moment the peaceful isolation seemed as far from the intensity of his business life as it was possible to be.

He was glad Claudia had brought him here.

It had meant a lot to him when she'd asked him to come

with her to the beautiful part of the world where her mother had grown up. Marco knew that her mother had died when she was just five years old—and that this place, with all its treasured memories, held a special place in Claudia's heart.

He turned away from the window to look down at her lying sleeping on the bed. Her long naked limbs were tangled in the sheets after hours of passionate lovemaking, and her hair was spread out in beautiful waves across the pillow. The gorgeous copper colour didn't show in the dark, but even in the moonlight her hair had a rich lustre and her perfect skin had a pearly luminescence.

As he gazed at Claudia, an unaccustomed feeling of warmth spread through him. They'd had a good day. It was an amazing place and Marco was touched that she'd wanted to share it with him—and that she'd already opened up her heart to him about something so personal and precious to her. And, although she was sad to have lost her mother when she was so young, it was wonderful to see the joy she was able to take from her memories.

Marco had not seen *his* mother for eight years—and his heart was full of anger and bitterness whenever he thought about her. She was a treacherous Jezebel who had allowed herself to be used against her own family, by a man called Primo Vasile—a corrupt and despicable con man of the very worst kind.

Then, after her treachery was complete—when the family had been utterly destroyed and Marco's father and grandfather were both dead—she had chosen to disappear. She had totally abandoned her eleven-year-old daughter, Marco's sister Bianca.

A band of tension tightened across Marco's chest, but he

shook his head sharply to clear his mind. He would *not* think about his mother and about what she had done eight years ago.

He would not let her ruin his perfect day with Claudia.

His mother's appalling betrayal had made it hard for him to completely trust anyone. And when his sister had introduced him to her new friend, Claudia, he had been wary of her at first.

Her family was involved with Primo Vasile—her father was one of Vasile's business partners—and that had been enough to make Marco suspicious. But, for his sister's sake, he'd taken the time to get to know her. And now he was glad that he had, because they had become so much more than just friends—more than the simple relationships he was used to with women.

As he looked down at her sleeping, he knew that the time he'd spent with Claudia was truly special.

Suddenly, the sound of his mobile phone vibrating on the bedside table broke into his thoughts. He sprang across the room and picked it up quickly so that it wouldn't disturb her.

'*Ciao*, Ricardo,' Marco said, slipping out of the small bedroom and walking down the narrow staircase to the living room below. 'Everything all right?'

It was very late at night, an unusual time for someone to call, and he'd felt an immediate rush of concern when he'd seen his friend's name on the caller display.

'Yes, everything's fine—at least it is now,' Ricardo said. 'But you should know, an hour ago I ran into Bianca at a party here in Turin. She was in trouble—'

'What happened? Is she all right?' Marco interrupted, fear for his now nineteen-year-old sister slamming into him like a sledgehammer.

'I hate to tell you this—but she was with Primo Vasile,' Ricardo said.

'Vasile!' Marco exclaimed, cursing savagely. What was *he* doing with his sister?

'She was very confused. I think he may have spiked her drink with something worse than alcohol.' Ricardo paused, clearly reluctant to say what he knew was going to cause his friend distress. 'When I came across them, he was asking her questions about your business and trying to get her to leave with him.'

Marco swore again, grinding his hand into a fist at his side.

'She's all right,' Ricardo reassured him. 'I got there in time.'

'Only just in time,' Marco bit out. 'That bastard's going to pay for this. Bianca is off limits—he should have known better than to try to get at me through her.'

'I *was* surprised to see her at a party organised by one of Vasile's PR agencies,' Ricardo said. 'I know how you feel about Vasile.'

'Are you telling me Vasile wasn't just a guest—that he was involved with the party?' Marco demanded, starting back up the stairs, two at a time, to the bedroom.

'I thought you knew—it was a publicity event for a new restaurant he's backing,' Ricardo said. 'I saw Claudia talking to him last week at the Miretti wedding.'

'What?' Marco stopped abruptly outside the bedroom door.

His blood ran cold and he felt the agonisingly familiar pain of betrayal slice into his guts like a vicious blade. His suspicions that Claudia might somehow be involved with the man who had destroyed his family had turned out to be true.

'I saw Claudia talking to Primo Vasile,' Ricardo said. 'I heard him tell her the time and place of tonight's party.'

For a moment Marco couldn't talk—he couldn't breathe.

The shattering truth of the situation knocked the breath right out of his body.

Claudia—his beautiful lover—had betrayed him. And her treachery had led Bianca into danger. Just like his mother, eight years ago, she had betrayed them both.

He pushed the door of the bedroom open and stared down at her. She was still sleeping—her face the image of angelic peace. Wasn't she at all concerned for her so-called friend—the girl who she'd sent into the jaws of the shark that evening?

'Marco, are you still there?' Ricardo asked.

'Yes, I'm here,' Marco said. 'I'm coming home at once—to take care of my sister.'

'What about Vasile?' Ricardo asked.

'I'll deal with him,' Marco said flatly. 'Thanks, Ricardo. You've been a good friend. I'll call you when I know what time I'll be back in Turin.'

He snapped his phone shut. It wasn't just Vasile who would feel the full force of his vengeance.

Claudia would also pay for what she had done—but not yet.

At that moment, his top priority was Bianca. He must make sure for himself that she was unharmed. He reached for his clothes and pulled them on. Then he put his wallet and his mobile phone in his pocket, picked up his bag and turned to leave.

He walked silently out of the room without a backwards glance.

CHAPTER ONE

Four years later

'MARRY you!' Claudia Hazelton gasped, too startled to mask her appalled reaction to the shocking proposal she'd just received. She set her cup down on her saucer with a clatter. 'You're not really asking me to marry you, are you?'

She was suddenly shaking like a leaf and her heart was pounding horribly, but she held her head high and forced herself to look straight across the beautifully laid table at the Ritz Hotel, into the face of the fifty-year-old man who had just proposed to her.

His name was Primo Vasile. He was her stepmother's cousin and her father's business partner. But, despite her family's connection to him, he had always made her skin crawl. There was no way in a million years she would ever consider marrying him.

'I'm not *asking* you,' Vasile said quietly, a nauseatingly smug expression on his smooth Italian face, 'I'm telling you. Or would you rather see your father face a criminal investigation and then go to prison for embezzlement of the company pension fund—if he even lives that long?'

Claudia stared at him in shock, horrified disbelief leaving her speechless for a moment. Surely Vasile could not really be saying that her father had stolen money from their joint business and that he expected Claudia to marry him, as a way of repaying that debt?

Suddenly, a painful image of her father lying critically ill in hospital flashed through her mind, pushing all other thoughts aside for a moment and making her throat constrict with grief. He was so frail and was already suffering terribly. She couldn't bear to think of him facing a criminal investigation or—even worse—prison.

But why was Vasile threatening that? She'd never liked him. But she couldn't believe he was actually trying to blackmail her into marriage.

'I don't understand why you are saying these awful things,' Claudia said. Her golden brown eyes were wide with confusion as she looked at him. 'Why would you want to hurt my father?'

'I don't *want* to hurt him,' Vasile said. 'But, if you don't accept my proposal, I may be forced to. He took a great deal of money, which needs to be repaid.'

'I can't believe my father would do something like that.' Claudia pushed her hair back from her stark white face with a jerky gesture and turned in appeal to her stepmother, who was sitting with them at the table.

They'd never been close. Francesca was not the type to let motherly responsibilities get in the way of her extravagant and self-indulgent lifestyle. But she must know the truth about the money—and surely even she wouldn't condone what her cousin was doing.

'I'm afraid it's true, darling. Marrying Primo is the only way to get us all out of this terrible mess,' Francesca said.

'When you are married, you will get access to your trust fund. We need that money to pay back what your father took from the company pension fund.'

Claudia bit her lip, trying to take in what they'd told her. The family business really must be in terrible trouble for things to have got this bad—bad enough for blackmail.

'There has to be another way,' Claudia said. 'I can help repay the debt.'

'Foolish girl!' Vasile scoffed. 'Apart from your trust fund—how could *you* ever raise the money needed?'

'I'll sell my flat and my car,' she replied. 'And maybe I could get a bank loan. I'll do whatever it takes—work as hard as I can to pay off the debt.'

'Don't be so naive!' The contempt in Vasile's voice clawed viciously across her nerves. 'We're talking about the pension fund here. Even *I* can't raise the amount of money needed. Hundreds of workers have paid contributions into that fund for years—and, if the money isn't replaced, they'll all lose their pensions.'

'How long will it be until the money is missed?' Claudia asked. She felt sick at the thought of all those loyal employees losing the income they were counting on for their retirement. She was sure her father could never have intended that innocent people should suffer—they had to find a way to put things right. 'What did my father do with the money? Surely we can get at least some of it back.'

'It's gone,' Francesca said. 'You must understand, darling—this really is the only way. You must marry Primo.'

'If we are not married by Christmas,' Vasile said, 'I'll be forced to go to the police.'

'Christmas!' Claudia gasped. 'It's already mid-December.

Why does it have to be so sudden? Why would you want to go to the police so quickly—surely you have some loyalty to my father after all this time?'

'Embezzlement is a serious crime,' Vasile said. 'If I'm not careful I'll be implicated too. I won't sacrifice myself to save your father.'

'You mean *you'll* have nothing left if my father's business goes under,' Claudia said. 'You're just trying to save your own skin.'

'It wouldn't be necessary if your father hadn't stolen the money,' Vasile sneered.

'I just can't believe my father could do such a thing,' Claudia repeated. She lifted her hands to cover her face for a second and let her long hair fall forward over her eyes. She closed them momentarily—still trying to come to terms with the fact that her father might have taken money that wasn't his.

'It's a bitter pill to swallow.' Vasile's heavily accented voice jarred intrusively in her ears, dripping with self-satisfaction. 'Your precious father is not so perfect after all.'

'I want to see proof. See the figures for myself,' Claudia said resolutely. It was unbearable that Primo Vasile was gloating over her father's mistake.

'No.' Vasile's voice was hard. 'There's no time for that.'

'Then I won't go through with it—not without proof that it's definitely necessary,' Claudia said. A wave of desperation rose up through her as she realised she might really have to marry Vasile to save her father from prison.

'Don't push your luck,' Vasile said, but he picked up his briefcase and pulled out a wad of documents. 'Here's your evidence—proof that your father ordered the money transfers into various private accounts.'

Claudia took the papers with a sinking heart. There, right in front of her eyes, were the documents to prove that her father had transferred company money into his own accounts. The numbers were huge—and there was a whole pile of transfer orders, each with her father's characteristic signature at the bottom.

'You're asking too much of me,' Claudia protested.

'No. Your father took too much,' Vasile said. 'And now *you* must give up the money he put in trust for you—if you want to save him from prison.'

'I don't care about the money!' Claudia brought her hands down to the table with a bang and her eyes snapped back up to Vasile's hateful face.

It was true that she didn't care about it. In her mind she had always associated the family wealth with personal loss—first the death of her real mother when she was just five years old and then her grandmother.

She'd never looked forward to her thirtieth birthday, when she was due to receive the money from her trust fund. It seemed so far away that she rarely thought about it. It had been her father's intention that by then she would have found her own way in the world. She would only receive the money earlier if she married. That was her father's way of providing for his grandchildren.

'Lower your voice,' Francesca hissed. 'Remember where we are.'

Claudia glared across the table at her stepmother. She looked so poised and confident.

A sudden, irrational jolt of irritation jarred through her. At that moment she hated Francesca's chic Italian style. Even now, when they were discussing something so important,

Francesca still looked as if she had stepped out of the latest edition of *Vogue*.

'Only *you* would bring us here,' Claudia said crossly, glancing round at the opulent cream and gold room. She knew Francesca felt at home surrounded by the sophisticated splendour of the Ritz Hotel—the clink of silver teaspoons against bone china and the gentle hum of conversation was comforting to her. 'Only you could blackmail your stepdaughter over afternoon tea at the Ritz!'

She looked down at the white tablecloth, wishing for the millionth time that her father had never married Francesca. But it wasn't his fault. He had been devastated by the death of Claudia's real mother and had been easy prey for the gold-digging Italian.

Even at seven years old, Claudia had not been fooled by Francesca. She'd instinctively seen through the Italian woman's fake charm and two-faced behaviour. But her father had been blinded by grief. Out of desire for companionship, and to provide a mother for his daughter, he had fallen into Francesca's trap. And with Francesca came her cousin, Primo Vasile, an unscrupulous businessman, keen to use Claudia's father—and his money—in any way he could.

'Blackmail?' Francesca echoed, looking almost genuinely bemused. 'No, no…it's nothing like that. It's just an arrangement that Primo has suggested in the interests of your father's health.'

'It's blackmail,' Claudia said frostily. 'Don't try to pretend it isn't.'

'No—' Francesca protested.

But Vasile lifted a hand to silence her. 'Claudia understands the situation,' he said, fixing her with his shrewd black eyes.

She shuddered. The sound of him saying her name and the way that he smiled at her made her stomach clench in revulsion.

'I will provide all the necessary paperwork,' Vasile continued. 'You just need to come to the Caribbean for our wedding and sign the documents that will keep your father from prison. Allow him to end his days peacefully in hospital.'

Claudia stared at Vasile in disgust, hardly able to believe the situation she had found herself in.

'There is one more thing,' Vasile added. 'Given the fact that your father is far too ill to talk, it's scarcely necessary to say this, but I must be absolutely clear on this point. You are never to discuss our arrangement with your father—or with anyone else. If you do, I will cut my losses by going to the police immediately.'

A flash of anger flared through Claudia at the cold-hearted way Vasile dismissed her father and at this extra barb he'd added to his blackmail—as if it wasn't hateful enough already.

Then, suddenly, all she could think about was how much her father was suffering. Her anger evaporated and her eyes filled with tears as she pictured him—his face a pallid grey next to the starched white hospital sheets as he drifted in and out of consciousness, his terrible pain and pitiful frailty showing whenever he was awake.

'It will be all right, darling,' Francesca said, startling Claudia by covering her hand with her own. 'There's no need to get upset.'

'My father is dying.' She paused, struggling to speak past the sadness that was closing her throat. 'How can you say it will be all right?'

'I meant we can keep him happy and comfortable,' Francesca said. 'Protect him from any more worries.'

Claudia pressed her teeth gently into her quivering lip, momentarily overwhelmed by a barrage of conflicting emotions.

She'd spent most of her life longing for a loving mother who could take care of her and comfort her when she was upset.

Now, for the first time she could remember, Francesca was trying to offer comfort. But, coming straight after joining forces with a man Claudia despised, with the purpose of blackmailing her into marriage, it was a hollow pretence.

'You don't care about him,' Claudia cried. 'You've never cared about him—you've only ever been interested in his money.'

Francesca withdrew her hand stiffly, but she did not respond to Claudia's impassioned comment.

'This will cheer you up,' she said, pulling a wedding dress brochure out of her designer bag. 'Just for inspiration, of course. After tea let's pop down to Harrods and see what they have.'

'I'm not going to Harrods to choose my wedding dress.' All Claudia wanted to do was get away on her own.

'Just for inspiration,' her stepmother repeated. 'Nothing off-the-peg for you, darling, but what do you think about something like this?'

Claudia looked at the fur trimmed December bride gracing the cover of the brochure.

'It's not exactly suitable for the Caribbean, is it?' She picked up her bag and was on her feet before she fully realised what she was doing. She couldn't bear to think of flying to the Tropics to present herself as a trophy bride to the despicable and vile Primo Vasile.

But the thought of her father ending his days in prison was absolutely unbearable. She would do whatever it took to spare him pain in his last few months of life.

'Where are you going?' Francesca asked. 'We have plans to make.'

'You don't need me to make plans,' Claudia said as she turned to leave. 'You just need me to carry them out for you.'

They said that revenge was a dish best served cold. And, as Marco De Luca waited outside the Ritz Hotel for Claudia Hazelton to appear, his heart felt as cold and hard as steel.

He stared straight ahead, oblivious to the hordes of Christmas shoppers thronging the streets in London's fashionable West End. He was completely disinterested in the Christmas lights that sparkled everywhere because, at any moment, Claudia would leave the hotel.

It was more than four years since he'd seen her, but he could still picture her face perfectly. Porcelain fair skin with a dusting of freckles. Fine bone structure and delicate features, framed by rich coppery hair that tumbled past her shoulders. Those large eyes that gave the appearance of angelic innocence.

But Marco knew Claudia was far from innocent. She had betrayed him and she'd made the unforgivable mistake of conspiring to hurt his sister.

And now, unbelievably, she planned to marry Primo Vasile—the man who had viciously ripped Marco's family to shreds twelve years earlier.

A knot twisted nastily in his stomach as he thought about Claudia and Vasile together. Their forthcoming marriage was utterly repellent to him—but it proved just how low Claudia was prepared to stoop. The only possible reason she could have for marrying a man like Vasile was to get her hands on her trust fund early.

Marco would make sure that marriage never happened.

A movement from the hotel's entrance caught his eye.

It was Claudia.

A sudden surge of unexpected emotion powered through him and his heart started to thud. Even though he'd been waiting for her, actually seeing her in the flesh hit him like a punch to the solar plexus.

He jerked into motion, falling into step behind her as she set off along Picadilly. She walked swiftly, weaving her way with single-minded determination through the crowds of Christmas shoppers filling the London street.

She looked every bit the sophisticated city woman, wearing a sleek chocolate-brown suede coat over tailored trousers and high-heeled boots. But in his mind's eye he suddenly saw her dressed in the faded T-shirt and old jeans she had worn the last day they'd spent together, trekking along the Pembrokeshire Coast Path.

He pictured her lying on the springy grass on the cliff top, the scent of wild thyme mingling with the sea breeze as he'd leant forward to kiss her. It had been an amazing day, for both of them he had thought, until he'd discovered it was all a smokescreen. She'd been deceiving him in the worst possible way—for the worst possible reasons.

'Claudia.' His voice caught in his throat and a strange sensation burned through him—a combination of the betrayal he'd felt when he'd discovered what she had done and the memory of the red hot passion they'd once shared. 'Claudia, is that you?' he asked, reaching out to lay his hand on her shoulder.

He felt her jump as his hand made contact, as if an electric shock had run through her.

'Marco.' His name formed soundlessly on her lips as she turned to face him, an expression of profound shock on her fine features.

She was even more beautiful than he remembered. In the

thin colourless light of the winter afternoon her skin glowed with almost ethereal paleness, but there was something achingly fragile about her that he didn't recall. His eyes roamed over her, trying to detect even the smallest changes in her appearance.

There were dark smudges under her eyes and her cheek-bones seemed more pronounced than before. But maybe it was simply knowing what he had planned for her that made her seem vulnerable to him.

Despite her elegant London grooming, she looked slightly dishevelled. Her gorgeous copper toned hair was caught up inside her collar, as if she'd thrown her coat on hurriedly, and his fingers longed to slip under its silken weight and ease it free.

Then, as she lifted her gaze to meet his, he found himself looking down into her golden brown eyes.

'Marco.' Claudia repeated his name out loud this time, hardly able to believe it as she stared up at his face. Her heart was racing and it was impossible to think straight.

It truly was him—Marco De Luca.

He had filled her thoughts for four long years and now he was really here, transported out of her dreams on to the London pavement beside her—except everything about the flesh and blood man was more vivid than the memory.

'I thought it was you,' he said. His voice tingled down her spine, deliciously deep and sexy, setting her quivering inside. 'I saw you walking.'

Claudia opened her lips and tried to speak again, but all she could think was how badly she'd missed him. He'd hurt her terribly when he'd dumped her four years ago, but he'd been in her thoughts every day since then. And now he was here, completely out of the blue, on what had seemed like the worst day of her life so far.

'Are you all right? You look like you've seen a ghost.' Curiosity glittered in his dark eyes as he looked down at her startled face. 'Have I caught you at a bad time? You appeared to be hurrying somewhere.'

All of a sudden, a wave of anger rose up and crashed through Claudia's initial shock at seeing him again. She drew in a deep breath, finding her voice at last.

'A bad time?' she demanded incredulously. He had broken her heart when he'd left her, but she'd never discovered the reason why he'd finished their relationship so abruptly. He hadn't even had the decency to tell her he was leaving. 'When would be a good time to run into an ex-lover—a man who dumped you without even bothering to tell you it was over?'

'Well...when you put it like that...' Marco paused, his wide expressive lips curling into a smile that took her breath away and swept through the ache that had filled her heart since the day he'd disappeared from her life.

'How would you put it?' she challenged him. 'Considering you walked out on me four years ago, without even telling me you were going.'

'I'd say how wonderful to see you, despite everything,' Marco said, holding her transfixed with his dark gaze. 'And what a fantastic opportunity to put things right between us.'

Claudia drew in a breath and tried to speak. She wanted to say that she wasn't naive enough to fall for his charming ways a second time. But she was caught by the power of his gaze. A sizzling, sensual energy was flowing between them, just as it always had. She felt it in every cell of her body. Every inch of her skin longed to be close to him. It was impossible to ignore.

'Then I'd say you're four years too late.'

Her voice sounded steady, but her body and mind were a churning mass of conflicting feelings. She took a hasty step away from him—as if putting a little distance between them would help her get a grip.

Making a sudden sideways move on the busy street was foolhardy and she felt someone crash heavily into her back almost immediately.

'Sorry!' A stocky man in a dark overcoat grunted as he put out his hands to steady himself.

'No…sorry…my fault,' Claudia gasped, trying to catch her breath. Then Marco's arms closed around her as he pulled her out of the flow of pedestrians into a shop doorway.

She stared up at him, thinking that he was still the most amazingly good-looking man she'd ever seen. From the moment they'd met, her attraction to him outstripped anything she'd ever experienced before.

When he'd turned his fathomless espresso coloured eyes on to her, it was as if she were the only woman in the world. She'd felt beautiful and special.

But she'd been a fool to let herself think that—things between them hadn't been what they'd seemed. He wasn't her soul mate. In fact, he'd shown just how little he cared for her when he'd discarded her so heartlessly.

'You seem out of place here, in all this hustle and bustle,' he said, tugging her closer to him as a group of people pressed past them into the London store they were sheltering beside. 'I'd rather be with you somewhere quieter—more private,' he added, tightening his hold on her.

Claudia looked at him, her heart beating erratically. He was holding her so close that she couldn't think clearly.

Secure in the powerful circle of his arms, her senses were going into overload. She could feel the warm strength of him, even through her winter coat, and her legs were brushing against his, sending little darts of awareness shooting through her.

The chemistry between them had always been incredible, but now she knew that chemistry was all it had ever been. If she'd known their affair had been meaningless to him—a casual fling that he could easily cast aside—she would never have got so deeply involved. She'd never have told him her secrets.

And she would never have fallen in love with him.

'I'm sorry,' Marco said. 'I've unsettled you by turning up like this.'

He moved to the side, breaking the contact between them to let another group of Christmas shoppers past. When he let go of her it felt like a rejection.

'It's not turning up unexpectedly that you should be apologising for,' Claudia said, the sting of losing physical contact with him making her voice sharper than she'd intended. 'What about the way you left me in the middle of the night, without bothering to tell me why? You didn't even have the decency to tell me to my face that it was over between us!'

'I do owe you an explanation,' Marco said. 'Let's go somewhere and talk.' His dark gaze slid down her in a way that made her think he wanted to do more than talk.

For a split second Claudia wondered what had made him call out her name when he'd spotted her in the street. He could easily have watched her walk away and she would have been none the wiser that they had passed by so close to each other. But now, the way his eyes were burning right through her clothes gave her an answer that made the pieces of her broken heart weep.

It was still just about sex.

And, shockingly, the look in his eyes told her that he wanted to pick up where they'd left off.

'It's too late for that,' she replied stonily, folding her arms resolutely across her chest.

Then suddenly the horrible realisation that she'd spoken the truth in more ways than one slammed into her like a lead weight. It was only a matter of days until she would have to marry Primo Vasile.

She slumped back against the shop window, hardly aware of the constant stream of shoppers brushing past her. Even if she was foolish enough to want to hear Marco's explanation, it made no difference what he had to say for himself. Because, even if her wildest dreams had come true and Marco had genuinely been in love with her, she could never be with him again.

Because she was committed to Vasile now. And if she didn't go through with her wedding to him, he would report her father's crime to the police.

'Let's get out of here,' Marco said, stepping close so that his broad shoulders shielded her from the crowd of people that had built up in the bottleneck of the shop doorway. Then he slipped his arm around her waist to guide her out into the street.

A shiver ran through her as he pulled her tight to his body and she drew in a shaky breath. For a moment the sheer pleasure of being held close to him took over, mercifully blotting everything else out.

But she wasn't in love with him any more. She couldn't be. No sensible, self-respecting woman would love a man after he'd dumped her so decisively. But the intervening time—and common sense—had done nothing to dull her physical awareness of him.

'Let me go.' She stopped suddenly, slipping out of his grip before he could react. Then she turned to look him straight in the eye. 'I don't want to hear what you have to say—it won't change anything.'

That was the simple truth—and the sooner she faced up to it the better. Whatever he said wouldn't change the fact that he had callously discarded her four years ago. And it wouldn't change the fact that she had to marry Primo Vasile.

'Then let's not talk about the past,' Marco said.

He stared down at Claudia's deceptively innocent face.

He wasn't surprised that she didn't want to discuss the night he'd left her in Wales—her reluctance to talk about it was further proof of her guilt. Another nail in her coffin.

It was obvious that he'd discovered she was in league with Primo Vasile. That she'd callously set Bianca up, then purposefully taken Marco out of the country to ensure his sister was alone and vulnerable.

His blood ran cold as he remembered the phone call he'd received from Ricardo that night in Wales. It had been a monumental stroke of luck that Marco's friend had come across Vasile and Bianca before something truly awful had happened.

'Let's not talk at all,' Claudia said, turning to walk away from him.

'Wait.'

A bolt of fury shot through him. He wasn't finished with her yet—how dared she walk away from him? He reached out and caught her arm, spinning her round so that they were face to face once more. He stared down at her and a strange feeling hit him in the chest.

Suddenly, it was as if he were seeing her for the first time.

He remembered only too well the afternoon that Bianca had introduced them. The minute he'd laid eyes on her at that high-society Turin wedding, he'd felt his blood quicken with desire. Dressed simply, with her long hair falling in natural waves around her shoulders and her pale English skin glowing in the Piedmont sunshine, she was a rare beauty. So refreshingly different from the chic Italian women he knew.

He had taken her slim hand in his and gazed down into her incredible eyes, experiencing an exquisite rush of pleasure as he'd anticipated getting to know her.

Then Bianca had told him her name.

Claudia Hazelton.

Like an unexpected icy wind scouring his skin, he had known at once who she was. Had known that eight years earlier her family had destroyed his.

But, as he'd started to talk to her, he'd been impressed by her openness and simple charm. He'd resolved not to judge her, based on a family background she'd had no control over, and he'd suppressed his natural suspicions of her, taking the time to get to know her.

It hadn't been long until they had fallen into bed, where he'd discovered to his great pleasure that she was a virgin. As the days had gone by, Marco had increasingly let down his guard, distracted by the extraordinary delights of spending time with her—making love and simply being together.

It was his sister who had paid the price.

Looking at Claudia now, standing on the busy London street, he knew that he'd never be fooled by her beauty or her charm again.

Her delicate face shone like an angel's in the dark and her

gorgeous copper hair, still caught inside the collar of her brown suede coat, was picking up rich multicoloured reflections from the Christmas lights.

She looked like an angel—but she was poison.

And she would pay for what she had done.

He lifted his hand and cupped her cheek, sensing a ripple of sensual awareness pass through her. That was the only thing between them that had been true—there was no way she could have faked her physical response to him.

Marco was going to taste the delights of her body one last time. But this time it would be on *his* terms. He knew now exactly what kind of woman she was and what she was capable of. And he would enjoy taking his revenge on her.

He let his fingers trail down the side of her neck, then slipped his hand underneath her hair. It was cool and heavy against the back of his hand, but her skin was hot under his palm. He felt her start trembling and a surge of potent desire powered through his body.

'I've been wanting to do this since I saw you,' he murmured, tipping his head to one side and leaning slightly closer.

Claudia stared up at him, almost mesmerised by the intensity of the expression on his face. He'd been gazing down at her for the longest moment and now she knew he was going to kiss her. She was sure of it.

The sultry tone of his voice had set her senses buzzing and her nerve-endings were already zinging where his hand touched her neck. But she knew she could not—must not—let him kiss her.

Then suddenly she felt him gently tugging her long hair, pushing the back of his hand against it and slowly pulling it free from where it was caught inside her coat.

It wasn't what she'd been expecting, yet somehow it felt intensely erotic. It was almost as if he were undressing her, teasing her body slowly out of a close-fitting, sexy garment. As the last strands of hair slipped free of her collar an uncontrollable shudder rippled through her. She couldn't mask her response. He'd seen it and felt it. All she could do was continue to gaze at him.

The moment stretched on but she couldn't break eye contact.

'The chemistry between us is still as hot as ever.' Marco spoke quietly, but his voice tingled across her body like a sensual caress.

Claudia could see the desire burning in his eyes and she felt her stomach tighten with the thrill of sexual anticipation.

Then, out of nowhere, a bubble of panic started to rise within her.

Suddenly nothing felt real. She couldn't believe that she was really standing there with Marco. She'd thought about him so many times over the last four years, desperately wishing things could have been different—wishing she could be with him.

But he had dumped her. Her heart had shattered into a million pieces and it had felt as if her life was over when he'd left. She'd be crazy to get involved with him again.

Besides, she didn't have only herself to think about now. Now there was her marriage to Primo Vasile. That didn't seem real either—it was more like a terrible nightmare—but she knew she had to go through with it. She couldn't do anything that might make Vasile take the incriminating information he had about her father to the police.

She would never forgive herself if her father was forced to face the humiliation of a criminal investigation and imprisonment. Not if there was anything—anything at all—that she could have done to prevent it.

'You're wrong. There's nothing between us,' Claudia said, pulling back, out of Marco's hold. 'I never want to see you again.'

Without giving him a chance to reply, she turned and fled.

Marco watched impassively as she ran away from him, quickly disappearing into the crowds of Christmas shoppers.

A slow smile spread across his cold face. That was quite a dramatic departure—he hadn't expected to have her running scared quite so soon. But it was of no matter.

She could run, but she couldn't hide from him.

CHAPTER TWO

CLAUDIA ran until she could run no more. Then she kept on walking, trying not to dwell on the complicated mess her life had suddenly become. Soon she'd have to face up to it—she had to travel to the Caribbean to marry Primo Vasile. But now, for just a couple of minutes, she needed to blot it out of her mind.

She wouldn't think about the appalling scene at the Ritz, when Vasile and her stepmother had blackmailed her. And she definitely wouldn't think about her encounter with Marco De Luca. It was far too distressing.

Instead, she found herself heading automatically towards the offices of the magazine she worked for, writing reviews of new digital cameras. She'd always intended to pop into work that evening to pick up a new model she was testing—and there was no reason to change her plan. She needed to cling on to normality—that way everything else didn't seem so bad.

That was how she had got through the last few months when her father, Hector, had become terribly ill. She'd visited him in Italy as much as she could, taking long weekends and using flexitime, then eventually she'd persuaded her boss to let her work from home for a while. But all the time she had been working hard, taking pride in her professionalism, she'd secretly known at the back of her mind that she was simply making a futile effort to keep life the way it was.

She'd been devastated by Hector's illness. He was her only living relative and she loved him dearly. She'd already lost her mother when she was just five years old, her beloved grandmother who had been so important to her throughout her childhood. Now her father was leaving her.

It seemed that *everyone* she loved eventually left her.

Even the only man she had ever loved, Marco De Luca, had left her.

Suddenly, the sound of someone calling her name caught her attention. It was her friend, Rosie, from work.

'What are you doing here so late?' her friend asked curiously. She was just leaving the building where the magazine had its offices.

'I came to collect a camera.' Claudia smiled warmly at her friend, despite the way she was feeling inside. 'What about you?'

'I've got a date later on and there wasn't any point going home first,' Rosie said. 'We're going ice-skating. Have you met my boyfriend, Rob?'

'I don't think so,' Claudia said, noticing that Rosie was following her back into the building. Although a large part of her wanted to be left alone right then, she knew instinctively that a little distracting company wouldn't hurt. 'Is he the tall, gorgeous one?' she asked, thinking of another man that description could equally well apply to.

'Yes.' Rosie grinned. 'Walk with me to Somerset House and I'll introduce you.'

'I'd love to,' Claudia said, 'but I don't think I'd be very good company this evening. I'm feeling really tired.'

'Come on,' Rosie said. 'You don't have to stay—actually, I'd prefer to keep him all to myself—but I just want to show him off!'

'All right—' Claudia laughed '—I promise I'll just admire him, then I'll take myself home and leave you two together.'

They walked down to The Strand, where an ice rink had been set up in the courtyard of the magnificent eighteenth century building of Somerset House. A giant Christmas tree was illuminated at one end of the rink and the ice was glittering under the sparkling coloured lights.

It wasn't long before Rosie's boyfriend arrived, then a few minutes later Claudia waved goodbye as they joined the queue for the next skating session.

She stood beside the railings for a moment, watching the skaters circling the rink. It was a beautiful scene, full of happy couples and families skating together.

Suddenly a wave of sadness washed over her. She felt more alone than ever before.

'You know where everything is,' Gwen said, handing Claudia the key to the old fisherman's cottage. 'Stay as long as you want—there's no one booked in till the New Year.'

'Thanks, Gwen,' Claudia said, leaning forward to kiss the eighty-year-old Welsh lady affectionately on the cheek. She was an old friend of her grandmother's, but she was still as sprightly as someone ten, or even twenty, years younger. 'I can only stay a night or two, but I just had to get out of the city for a little while.'

'Should I call Rhys to give you a lift down the hill?' Gwen asked in her wonderful accent.

'No thanks. My bag isn't heavy,' Claudia said, turning to

leave. She didn't want to bother Gwen's son, Rhys. He must be close to retirement age, but she'd seen him busy working in his vegetable garden as she'd walked from the bus stop. 'After the train and bus, I could do with some fresh air.'

'Plenty of that here,' Gwen laughed as she wrapped her woolly cardigan tightly around herself and closed her front door.

Claudia hefted her bag on her shoulder and set off along the winding road that led down to the cottage. She'd been coming to this part of Wales all her life and it was like a second home to her. In fact, until her grandmother died when she was thirteen, it had felt more like her home than the pristine town house she'd lived in with her father and Francesca.

Gwen had been her grandmother's friend and neighbour for sixty years. After her grandmother died, Gwen had extended a permanent invitation for Claudia to visit whenever she wanted. Gwen and her son Rhys owned a little cottage that they rented out to holidaymakers for a bit of extra income, but whenever it wasn't booked Claudia was welcome to stay in it.

It was mid-afternoon by the time she got to the cottage and, as she wanted to fit in an hour's work before it got dark, she grabbed her camera and headed straight down to the sea.

It was good to be back in Wales. It was the one place in the world where she felt a strong connection with her mother. Maybe here, far away from all her troubles, she might find some much needed peace of mind—if only for a day or two before she gave herself over to Francesca and Vasile's unthinkable scheme.

It was at this cottage that Marco had left her four years ago, and she'd briefly wondered whether it was wise to come here and risk stirring up memories. But it was already too late—meeting Marco yesterday had seen to that.

Besides, she'd been to the cottage lots of times since he'd left, and right now the blustery conditions couldn't have been more different from the glorious summer weather they had enjoyed when she'd brought Marco to her mother's home village.

The water foamed around the slick black boulders as she carefully picked her way out across the rocky beach towards the incoming tide. The water was already filling the deeper recesses between the rocks and she had to tread carefully so as not to slip. She knew there was still plenty of time to make it out to her favourite vantage point—a particularly giant rocky mound that stood higher than the surrounding beach.

It felt good to be working. For a few minutes she could put all her troubles out of her mind and concentrate on taking photos. Photography had always been her passion. She felt so fortunate that her job included taking photos to assess how each camera performed in different conditions.

The sky was low with dark clouds and the churning sea was a deep slate grey with an ever-moving pattern of white water as the waves broke across the rocks. A strong wind whipped her hair about and roared in her ears, combining with the sound of the crashing waves to create a wild, atmospheric soundtrack. It was a dramatic scene—and it suited her mood.

But, despite her efforts to clear her mind, Claudia's thoughts turned to Marco. She bit her lip and stared out across the bay, but she wasn't seeing the view. She was remembering how devastated she'd been when Marco had left her.

She'd woken up early in the morning, the thin dawn light filtering through the curtains in the cottage bedroom, to find him gone. At first she'd been frantic with worry, imagining something terrible had happened to him. But then she'd realised that his sports car was gone and he'd packed and taken all his things with him.

Then she'd remembered he'd received a phone call late in the evening. At the time she hadn't thought anything of it. He had always worked, day and night, and phone calls had been an inevitable part of that. But, when she'd thought about it, she didn't remember him coming back to bed afterwards—she must have fallen into a deep sleep after hours of lovemaking that evening, and had been oblivious to him packing and leaving.

She'd started to worry that he'd received terrible news, that maybe his sister had been in an accident or perhaps there'd been an incident at one of the businesses he owned.

But she'd never found out what had happened.

His mobile phone had been switched off, then later on the number had been discontinued. His PA had changed immediately to someone she didn't know—a brisk Italian woman who'd stonewalled all her attempts to contact him by any method.

She tried to get in touch with Bianca, but her number had been changed too. Eventually, the only information she ever received to explain what happened, was a brief text message from Bianca, saying that Marco was taking her to America, to set her up with contacts in the fashion industry.

And that was it.

After a while Claudia had been too upset to try any more. It was clear that she hadn't been anything more to Marco than a summer fling. He had broken her heart and it had taken a long time to heal. Maybe it had never healed.

But Bianca had hurt her too. She'd thought they were friends, but the nineteen-year-old girl had been quick enough to drop her when exciting new opportunities arose.

Claudia shook her head decisively. She wouldn't dwell on the past. She took a deep breath of the fresh sea air, lifted the camera and concentrated on the task in hand. She was here to work.

She told herself firmly that the tumultuous conditions were perfect for some excellent shots, with huge waves rolling in and crashing spectacularly over the jagged rocks. Although the afternoon light slanting down in erratic bursts through the gaps in the clouds would be challenging.

Marco De Luca strode purposefully across the meadow that led down to the beach. He frowned as he glanced around, disconcerted by how familiar everything looked—the rocky beach, the spectacularly eroded dark grey limestone outcrops that flanked the bay and even the rickety wooden stile that led to the cliff path.

It was more than four years since Claudia had brought him here, and it was winter now rather than summer, yet for some reason he seemed to recall everything with absolute clarity.

He'd been surprised by how easily he'd found the old fisherman's cottage but, as he'd wound his sports car through the maze of narrow farm lanes, he'd remembered exactly which turnings to take.

Claudia had not been at the cottage, so he'd come to the beach to look for her. He reached the edge of the shingle and paused to scan the small bay. It was cold and damp and, as the light was starting to fade, he guessed Claudia couldn't be far away. Despite her love of the outdoors, she wouldn't want to get caught on the beach or cliff path after dark. There were no street-lights here and, with the amount of cloud cover, it seemed unlikely there'd be much moonlight either.

It only took him a couple of moments to spot her, perched on top of a rocky mound that appeared to be surrounded by the sea. He realised she was taking photographs and started walking towards her.

Suddenly he was taken aback by the familiarity of her body language. Although she was quite a distance from him, and was crouched down looking out to sea, he knew with complete certainty what expression would be on her face. He could tell she was lost in her craft, only aware of the dramatic seascape in front of her and how it appeared through the lens of her camera.

That meant there would be a faraway look on her beautiful face. Her brow would be smooth and relaxed and she'd hardly notice as her hair blew in her almond shaped eyes, catching in her exquisitely long eyelashes.

He stopped abruptly and his dark eyes narrowed dangerously as he stared at her. What was he doing, letting his thoughts run away like that? He started striding purposefully towards her once more. Then, for the second time in as many minutes, he was suddenly brought up short again. It didn't just look as if Claudia was surrounded by the sea—she really *was* cut off.

A bolt of alarm shot through him. The incoming tide had got the better of her while she had been distracted by her photography. And so far she still seemed completely oblivious to her perilous situation.

Foolish girl! He cursed her angrily and broke into a run, quickly assessing the terrain between them for the highest, safest route out to her. The black rocks were slick with sea water washing over them and were interspersed with deep, ankle-turning crevices that he had to avoid.

'Claudia!' He shouted her name, but the wind swept his voice away and she did not turn towards him.

Running as fast as he safely could, it didn't take long to reach her. Then, as he splashed through knee-deep water foaming on the platform of rock that surrounded her vantage point, he knew he'd only just been in time. The water was continuing to rise with each new wave that crashed towards the beach.

He called her name again and this time she heard it. He saw her jolt back to her senses and she whipped round to look at him.

'Marco!' She stared at him in shock, then almost at once an expression of anger descended over her face. 'What are you doing here? Did you follow me?'

'Come on!' Marco shouted above the sound of the crashing waves and held out his hand to her.

'I'm not going anywhere with you!' she exclaimed furiously. 'How dare you follow me here—you had no right!'

'There's no time to mess about—look around you!' Marco barked, stepping closer and reaching up to seize her arm. 'We're about to get cut off by the water.'

As Marco's hand closed round her forearm, Claudia automatically pulled back against him, trying to shake him off. Then suddenly his words sank in.

Her eyes widened with alarm as she looked around, finally taking in the situation. The tide was coming in fast and she was surrounded. Marco, standing up to his knees in the churning water, was reaching up and trying to pull her down from her rock.

Anger that he had followed her to Wales still filled her, but now a surge of adrenaline mixed with it. If she didn't move quickly she would be completely stranded and even the rock she was perched on would be submerged as the tide reached its maximum height.

But she did not need Marco's help.

She jumped to her feet, jerking her arm out of his grip, and slid off the rock. The water felt freezing as it flooded into her boots. Then a wave hit her legs, knocking her off balance, and she stumbled backwards, bashing the camera that was clutched in her hand into the rock.

'Come on,' Marco snapped, seizing her arm and pulling her towards the shore. 'There isn't much time before we'll be in serious trouble.'

'Let go of me!' She pulled her arm out of his grip again and started heading inland. It was almost impossible to see through the swirling water and she inched forward, feeling her way carefully with her feet. 'I don't need your help.'

Suddenly a particularly strong wave crashed into the back of her legs, making her stagger forwards. She plunged down into the cold, salty sea and felt her hand slide off the edge of the boulder they were standing on, into the deep water surrounding it. She sucked in a frightened breath, knowing she was about to dive headlong into the chasm between the rocks.

The next instant the water closed terrifyingly over her head. She flailed around in panic, trying to find something to grip on to. Then, a split second later, she felt herself being hauled upright.

Her heartbeat pounded in her ears and water streamed down her face. For a moment she didn't know what had happened—then she realised Marco had saved her. She was still trying to catch her breath, but he was already pulling her towards the shore again.

'We have to keep going,' he said, his arm clamped tightly round her.

Claudia started moving through the water once more, but the waves continued to tug mercilessly at her legs. She was shaking from the shock of what had happened and it was hard to keep up with the fast pace Marco was setting.

Suddenly he turned and swept her up into his arms.

'Put me down!' she protested, automatically fighting his grasp.

'Lie still!'

His voice shot through her, somehow compelling her to obey, and she stopped struggling immediately. Marco's arms were strong and his body powerful, and the panic that had filled her when she'd plunged beneath the water gradually subsided.

The waves pushed and pulled around his legs, occasionally making his stride uneven, but Claudia felt secure. It didn't take long to reach the edge of the water. But, when he didn't put her down, she realised that he planned to carry her right across the beach to the meadow beyond. The dark grey shingle crunched and shifted beneath his feet and she felt him instinctively tighten his hold on her.

As his powerful muscles flexed, she suddenly became completely aware of his body. She was no longer distracted by the sea swirling around them, and she noticed every movement he made as he walked. She could sense the muscular strength of his chest and feel the resilient power in his legs as he carried her over the unstable shingle. She could feel the heat radiating off him, passing straight through the cold sea water that had soaked them both. It was as if a physical, sensual connection was growing between them.

Her heart started to beat faster and, despite the cold, she felt a flush rise to her cheeks. The next moment they reached solid ground and Marco dumped her unceremoniously on to her feet.

'What the hell were you doing?' He launched straight into her, gripping her upper arms and looking at her in a way that demanded an instant response.

She stared at his furious expression in shock and pushed

her dripping hair back from her face with a small, jerky gesture that was restricted by the way he was holding her so tightly. His brows were drawn low, making his eyes appear almost black with anger, and his lips were pulled into a fierce line.

A flash of irritation whipped through her. What did *he* have to be so angry about? What made him think he could sweep in and start manhandling her, acting as if she had to answer to him for something that was none of his business?

'What was *I* doing?' she asked incredulously, trying in vain to shrug her arms out of his iron grip. 'What about *you*— what are *you* doing here? Why did you follow me to Wales?'

'Didn't you realise it was nearly high tide?' he demanded, totally ignoring her questions and giving her a little shake that sent droplets of water flying from her hair.

'I knew the sea was coming in—but I was working,' she said, trying to sound as if she'd known exactly what she was doing when in fact she'd been shocked to see just how high the water had risen. 'You get better photos that way. The splashes are bigger. There's more dynamic energy in the water.'

She pulled back again but he tightened his grip, suddenly making her ultra-aware of his hands on her arms. The rest of her body was still cold and wet but, where his hands touched, a fiery heat was burning through her sodden clothes and penetrating the flesh beneath.

'For God's sake!' Marco exclaimed. 'You were cut off.'

'You didn't need to come out to get me,' she said crossly, pulling her arms sharply out of his grip and stepping away from him.

She wobbled slightly, but she held her head high. She did not need to explain herself to him—and she wasn't going to let herself be distracted by the feel of his hands.

'You could have been swept away,' he said harshly. 'What would have happened if I hadn't been here?'

'I'm a good swimmer. And I can clamber over rocks just like anyone else,' she said. 'I didn't ask you to come out to get me. And I didn't need you to carry me!'

'Swimming doesn't come into it—not with those white horses pounding you!' he exclaimed, gesturing fiercely towards the huge white crested waves that were breaking over the rocks.

Claudia turned and stared at the wild sea with startled eyes. Suddenly her head was spinning and her legs felt weak. But it wasn't the power of the waves that was roaring in her ears and making her dizzy. It was hearing Marco describe them as 'white horses'.

She had taught him that phrase.

Four years ago when she'd brought him to Pembrokeshire—to the tiny village where her real mother had grown up—she had told him how much she loved to photograph a stormy sea. The weather had been beautiful as they'd sat together on the headland, looking out over the mirror-flat surface of the bay. On that day it had been almost impossible to imagine the sea anything other than a tranquil backdrop to a perfect summer's day.

Claudia had been so happy. So in love. She'd looked deep into Marco's eyes and he had pulled her close to him. His lips had found hers and they'd tumbled down on to the springy thyme-scented grass, totally lost in each other.

But she had given her heart—and her body—to nothing more than a fantasy. Marco's feelings for her had not been real. He had used her and discarded her. That exact same night, Marco had walked out while she had been sleeping—without bothering to tell her he was going, or even to leave her a message.

'Claudia—' Marco's voice, hard and insistent, broke into her reverie and brought her hurtling back to the present '—you're shivering!'

She stared at him with wide eyes.

He was right—she was shivering. But whether it was from the cold, or the shock of plunging into the sea, or from the unexpected force of her memories she couldn't say.

'Why did you follow me to Wales?' she demanded—repeating the question he had evaded earlier. Her voice caught in her throat as she spoke, but she needed to know the answer. 'How did you even know I was here?'

'Your friend at work told me,' he said.

'You mean Rosie?' Claudia looked up at him in surprise. 'She shouldn't have done that. And you had no right to go behind my back, asking questions about where I was.'

'Why not—I wanted to see you,' he responded. 'To talk to you.'

She stared at him, knowing it couldn't really be that simple. No one followed another person that far just to talk to them. There must be something else. He must want more.

He was standing with his back to the sea and she could hear the waves crashing dramatically on to the rocky beach behind him. It was an unfamiliar, wild and stormy setting for them to be together. Their brief, intense affair had taken place during the summer, mostly in the elegant and stylish northern Italian city of Turin—and that was where she'd usually thought of him.

But somehow Marco's raw masculine presence seemed to fit the untamed beach in the wilds of Pembrokeshire perfectly. His clothes were soaked through, his black hair was spiky with salt water, and the edgy, slightly dangerous quality that usually characterised his expression seemed to echo their elemental surroundings exactly.

'If you knew where I worked, why didn't you just leave me a message?' she asked, suddenly feeling unnerved by the brooding sexual energy that glinted in his dark eyes.

She wrapped her arms across her body and hugged herself tightly. It was an instinctive gesture, as much about defending herself from Marco's penetrating gaze as about keeping warm. But he had seen her reaction to him, and his eyes glittered all the more.

'Oh, but I forgot—you don't *do* messages,' she added quickly, determined to stand up for herself and not let the sheer force of his personality overwhelm her.

'I couldn't wait that long.' He was unfazed by her barbed comment and deliberately let his eyes drift down across her body, leaving a sudden flare of heat where they passed. 'I needed to see you—now.'

'Why?'

But Claudia already knew the answer. And if the potent message in his dark and meaningful gaze wasn't enough, his voice had dropped to a sensual purr that shimmied across her body like a lover's caress.

'After you'd gone, I couldn't get you out of my mind,' he said.

His eyes burned into hers and Claudia knew exactly what he was thinking about. And that was enough to fill her own mind with powerful images of Marco making love to her.

But it was not what she wanted. Although her pulse was racing and the deep, dark longing to lie in Marco's arms again was making it hard to think straight—the thought that he had followed her all the way to Wales simply to bed her was utterly crushing.

Was that really all she'd ever been to him—someone to warm his bed? Didn't he care enough about her to ask how she'd been since he'd left her? Of course not. If he cared at all, he would never have left her so heartlessly.

Terrible tremors ripped through her body, making the shivering that had gripped her even more intense. But it wasn't just the cold and wet of her physical condition that was affecting her—it was the brutal reminder of just how little she'd meant to Marco.

'We have to get you out of those wet clothes,' he said, suddenly closing the distance between them. Then, before she could react, he lifted her up again and started striding across the meadow to the cottage.

'Put me down!' Claudia gasped, struggling against him. The idea of him undressing her flashed through her mind in a series of erotic images which aroused and scared her at the same time. 'I said, put me down!'

'We need to warm you up right away,' he said, his voice showing no sign of effort as he hurried towards the cottage. 'You're soaked through—we stood in the cold wind too long.'

As Marco held her tight against his chest, he was shocked by just how hard she was shaking. He could even hear her teeth chattering.

He didn't know much about hypothermia. A dip in the December sea obviously wasn't ideal, but he wouldn't have thought she'd be at serious risk that quickly. However, she was shivering so intensely that an unpleasant jolt ran through him and settled like a wedge of ice in his chest. He could not let anything happen to her!

'Stop struggling!' he barked. 'If you catch your death of cold, you'll be no good to anybody.'

His voice sounded harsh even to his own ears and he felt
his heart pound with concern beneath his ribs. But he schooled
his features into a blank expression and crammed the unwanted emotion back into submission.

It was *not* fear for Claudia's well being that had made him
react so strongly. If she was laid up with the flu, it could ruin
everything.

He hurried towards the cottage, cursing her for foolishly
letting herself be overtaken by the tide. How she had survived
twenty-five years of life when she showed so little concern
for her own personal safety, he couldn't fathom.

She was normally a streetwise and savvy young woman,
well able to look after herself. But the way photography
totally absorbed her, blotted out her common sense and awareness, had always made him uneasy. He remembered with
sickening clarity the day he'd feared she would fall from the
cliff as she'd slid on her stomach nearer and nearer to the
crumbling edge, concentrating on getting the perfect shot of
fledgling kestrels around their nest on a ledge below her.

He shook his head sharply, angrily rejecting the vivid
memory. He would not think about the past. It was not
possible to separate memories of what they had done
together—things at the time he thought he'd enjoyed—from
the knowledge that it had all been a lie. That she'd duped him
into trusting her. And then she had betrayed him.

'Where is the key?' His voice was as hard as steel as they
reached the cottage.

Claudia looked up at him, momentarily dazed, and struggled to pull her thoughts together—the icy cold was numbing
her mind as well as her body.

'P…p…pocket…' she said. 'P…put me down.'

Marco set her down on her feet on the doorstep and she tried to slide her hand into the pocket of her jeans. But she was still shivering and clumsy and she couldn't seem to get her fingers past the stiff denim.

'Let me.'

She had barely registered the words when suddenly Marco pushed her hand impatiently aside. A moment later his fingers delved deeply and forcefully into the tight pocket of her jeans.

It was over in a moment and he was already inserting the key into the lock before she fully realised what was happening. Her mind might be feeling numb—but her body had responded instantly to the intimate invasion of her personal space.

Shocking desire for him rolled through her, weakening her will to resist him. But, as he stepped towards her, looking as if he planned to pick her up again, she forced herself to dodge out of his reach.

'I can walk on my own.' She tried to dash inside, but her legs were wobbly and Marco easily kept pace with her. She had no chance of running ahead and reaching the sanctuary of the bathroom before him. No chance of closing the door and locking him out.

He strode past her and turned on the shower. Then his attention switched back to her.

'I'm all right now,' she said, feeling a ripple of apprehension pass through her as she looked at his intent face. 'You can go.'

'You're shaking too much to undress yourself,' he said, looking at her with his eyes narrowed in assessment.

She drew in a breath and started to protest, but he ignored her attempts to knock his hands away from her body and pulled off her coat and fleece before she could stop him. He dumped them in a soggy pile on the tiled floor and reached for her again, but at last she found the strength in her shaky legs to move decisively away from him.

'Then I'll warm up in the shower with the rest of my clothes on.' She spoke with conviction, wrapping her arms across her stomach and holding her T-shirt tightly in place. 'They're already wet.'

She let out a shaky breath as he stepped away from her, but then her eyes widened in surprised agitation as he started to strip off his own clothes. Watching his fluid movements as he removed his coat and sweater made her heart begin to patter. Wild thoughts flicked through her mind— how many more clothes would he remove? What did he plan to do next?

Then, before she realised what he was about, he knelt down to unlace their boots. A moment later he lifted her bodily into the shower, stepped in beside her and pulled the screen closed behind him.

'This should get your blood flowing again.'

He adjusted the temperature of the water slightly, then took hold of her upper arms to manoeuvre her so that the water hit the back of her neck and streamed down over her shoulders, warming as much of her body as possible.

'There isn't room for two,' she said irritably, lifting her head slightly to look at him—trying not to wonder if he meant the hot water would get her blood flowing or if he was referring to showering together.

She pressed herself back against the tiled wall, creating as much distance between them as possible in the small space.

'We've shared this shower before,' he said, letting her know that his thoughts had followed the same path. 'There seemed to be enough room then—although you weren't quite so preoccupied with maintaining a safe distance between us on that occasion.'

'Things have changed,' Claudia said.

In her mind she knew that was true—but her body still didn't seem to have accepted it and was responding in the way it always had to the thrilling proximity of Marco's unalloyed masculine presence.

He was standing with his back against the tiles, away from the falling water, but he was soaked through. His black T-shirt hugged the hard muscled form of his powerful chest and shoulders, making her completely aware of his pure physical strength.

He was absolutely still, apart from the rise and fall of his chest as he breathed, but Claudia sensed danger. He looked so big and powerful, like a black leopard watching his prey. His jet-black hair and T-shirt were in stark contrast to the clean white tiles behind him, and the darkness of his silhouette somehow added to his menacing presence.

They were not touching, but they were impossibly close, making her almost afraid to breathe too deeply in case the slight movement was enough to bring them into contact.

Vivid images of the last time they had shared that shower stormed through Claudia's mind, almost like a sexy movie playing out. Except it wasn't just pictures in her mind—she could remember the sensations that had rolled through her body when he'd touched her and now she could hear the sound of her own breathing growing heavier as she grew more and more aroused.

The shower water was streaming over her body with considerable force and it was easy to imagine that the sensation of the water washing over her, penetrating her clothing and stroking her most intimate places, was really the touch of Marco's hands.

Her breasts were straining against the confines of her bra, heavy with their need to be caressed. Her nipples were tingling sensual peaks that longed to feel the heat of Marco's mouth, to enjoy the bliss he could bring with the skilful movements of his tongue against her throbbing flesh.

Her whole body was still humming with pent-up desire for him, even though she instinctively knew she should be wary of him. She ought to put up defences. She should stop herself remembering all the times they had made love in the past. But it was totally beyond her intellectual control. The innermost part of her being remembered what it was like to make love with Marco and wanted to experience those soaring heights again.

'You're still shaking.' His words made her jump and her eyes flew back up to his face. 'Are you all right?'

'I'm fine,' Claudia said, desperately trying to keep her voice steady. She could not let him guess what she had been thinking about. 'I'll be okay on my own now.' If only he would step out of the shower she'd be able to get herself back under control. Even if that meant she had to turn the water temperature right down.

'You haven't warmed up yet,' Marco said, letting his gaze slide lower across her body.

'Yes, I have. Really.' She tried to sound confident—come across as certain of what she was saying. But all she could think about was how the touch of his eyes was almost as potent as the touch of his hands. Her body was positively buzzing with the desire to get closer to him. 'You should get out of the shower now,' she added.

'You don't look warm. You're still shaking and...' He

paused, looking at her body with a burning intensity that made Claudia's stomach turn over.

She dipped her head, following his line of vision, and looked down at herself. Her nipples were clearly visible, jutting pert and sexually aroused against the almost transparent cotton of her saturated top.

'Oh!' she gasped, automatically lifting her hands to press them over her breasts, but not before she'd felt the full force of his gaze caressing her, making her nipples burn with need.

Embarrassment surged through her and she kept her head bowed, willing him to move away. Suddenly he lifted his hand and cupped it under her chin, tilting her head up so that he could look into her eyes.

'It's not the cold that's making you tremble.' His voice was deep and sexually loaded, his Italian accent more pronounced than usual.

She stared up at him, wanting to deny what he'd said. But she knew it was pointless—he'd never believe her. It was a long time ago, but they *had* been lovers—passionate lovers. He knew her body well, and from the very beginning of their affair he'd been able to take her to unimaginably wonderful heights that she had never dreamed possible.

But now, for so many reasons, she could not let it happen again.

'Thank you for getting me back to the cottage…and for the shower,' she said. 'But I'm okay now. I'm going to get changed.'

She turned to get out of the shower but, as she did so, Marco moved too. With one step he blocked her way and at the same time his hands closed on her waist, pulling her tight to him, so that their thighs brushed together and her nipples pressed against his chest.

'We haven't finished yet.' His voice rumbled through her with a sexual promise so potent that it started an insistent throbbing at the very core of her.

'There isn't room to shower properly together.' She struggled to pretend everything was perfectly normal, but the heat radiating off his powerful body didn't make things any easier. 'You take first turn—I'll shower later.'

'You already made it plain you didn't rate my heroic rescue,' Marco said, humour mixing with the rich sensual tones that already coloured his deep voice. 'But is taking first turn in the shower to be my only reward?'

'I'll be more comfortable on my own,' Claudia insisted, trying not to think about the feel of his hands burning on her waist, or her tingling nipples brushing tantalizingly against his chest.

'Comfort isn't what you're after—not the girl who was perched precariously on a boulder above the sea with a wild tide coming in,' he drawled. 'No, I think you were looking for a little excitement.'

'Not the kind of excitement you're talking about,' she responded, already feeling her speeding pulse crank up an extra notch. 'We've done that before, and it didn't work out.'

'Didn't work?' he purred, leaning close to her ear so that his breath mingled with the droplets of shower water that were still splashing on her neck. 'Are you telling me you weren't satisfied with my lovemaking?'

'That's not what I said,' Claudia managed to say, feeling her cheeks blaze.

'So you were satisfied?' he said, tugging her closer still. 'I thought so.'

'We can't go there again,' she said, trying to pull away from him, but he was so effortlessly strong that physical resistance was futile. She had to rely on her wits, which were totally addled by the feelings of desire that were engulfing her.

'Why not?' he asked, slipping his hands under the hem of her top. She drew in her stomach muscles instinctively, letting out a long shuddering breath as his fingers skimmed over her skin. But then he took hold of the fabric, as if he was about to pull the top up and over her head.

'No. Please don't take my clothes off.' Her voice was no more than a whimper, husky with blatant sexual desire. Even to her own ears it sounded more as if she'd said, *Please, rip off all my clothes and ravish me right here and now.*

To her surprise, and sudden crushing disappointment that was totally out of the realm of sensible thought, he let go of her top, leaving her fully dressed. Then, in one fluid movement, he divested himself of his own T-shirt.

'Oh!' she gasped and stared at his naked chest. The sight of his golden skin, slick with water droplets, made her mouth run dry. She swallowed hard, overwhelmed by just how much she wanted to reach out and slide her hands over the muscular expanse of his chest.

She closed her eyes and leant back against the tiled wall of the shower, inadvertently passing her head directly under the full force of the gushing water. She reached up to wipe her eyes, trying not to think about the magnetic lure of his perfect masculine form, when suddenly she heard a sound that could only be Marco undoing the zip of his trousers.

Her eyes flew open in time to see him stepping free of the garment, so that he was standing next to her wearing nothing but a pair of black silk boxers. The fine fabric was so wet that it clung to his proud, viral form intimately, leaving virtually nothing to her imagination.

'You may want to shower with your clothes on,' Marco said. 'I find I'm more *comfortable* without them.'

CHAPTER THREE

A SLOW, sensual smile spread across Marco's face as he watched Claudia's reaction to him stripping off.

A misty veil of steam surrounded her, softening her features in an utterly alluring way, but that didn't hide the flash of pure desire that lit her golden eyes, or the rapid rise and fall of her breast as she started breathing even more quickly than she had been a moment before.

He knew that it wouldn't take much to shatter her control. If he pulled her roughly into his arms, giving free rein to the passion that was surging through his body, it would only be a matter of moments before she surrendered to him and to her own growing desire.

But simply making love to Claudia was not his ultimate goal. He wanted to make her trust him, as he had trusted her before she'd betrayed him. And he wanted to make her desperate for him—physically. Sexually.

'I've missed you,' he said, taking her face in his large, warm hands and kissing her quickly on the mouth.

A powerful feeling ripped through him, although he couldn't have identified what emotion it was, and he suddenly found that the words he'd chosen with the intention of drawing her in were closer to the truth than he would care to admit, even to himself.

'Why did you follow me to Wales?' She repeated the question she'd asked on the beach one more time, staring up at him with wide eyes, filled with a mixture of confusion and undisguised sexual need.

'I told you—I wanted to see you again.' He lifted a hand to smooth a lock of wet hair back from her face and he felt a tremor run through her. But he knew she wanted to hear that it was more than just desire for her that had made him follow her. 'I've thought about you every day we've been apart.'

She was standing bolt upright in the shower, with water pouring down over her shoulders and across her breasts, but she seemed completely oblivious to her surroundings and was looking at him intently, hanging on every word.

'After you'd gone yesterday I couldn't get you out of my mind.' He smiled and brushed his thumb gently across her cheekbone.

'It's a long way to come on a whim.' Claudia looked up at him, wishing she knew for sure why he had come to the cottage.

'In the circumstances, I think it was lucky I came,' he replied.

She thought back to the beach. An involuntary shudder ran through her. Despite her earlier denials, she knew she'd had a lucky escape from the incoming tide. And she had Marco to thank for that.

'I could have been sucked down between those rocks when I fell,' she said, remembering the panic that had filled her when the cold water closed over her.

'No,' Marco said. 'The gap wasn't big enough. Most likely you would have bashed your head on the rock. Knocked yourself unconscious.'

She stared up at him in startled silence, suddenly too frightened to think about what might have happened.

'It's all right.' Marco's voice was suddenly gentle as his hand slipped round to the nape of her neck. 'No harm done.'

She watched him lean closer and bend his head towards hers. The steam from the shower made everything appear to be in soft focus, but she was acutely aware of every single movement he made. The way he was tipping his head slightly to one side, the way his sensual lips were slightly parted. The way his mouth was getting closer and closer to hers.

Then, after a never-ending moment of anticipation, his lips brushed hers. Tantalizingly light, the delicate contact set her lips tingling with a yearning desire for more. Without realising what she was doing, she rose to her tiptoes and tried to kiss him properly.

But Marco was in control of the kiss. His hands cradled her face, holding her securely—right where he wanted her to be. He pulled away slightly, teasing her, and a long low sigh escaped her. She closed her eyes, aching for him to kiss her again.

At last his mouth closed over hers. A ripple of delight spread through her body and she felt herself dissolving into a pool of bliss.

He kissed her slowly, his lips moving gently against hers. His tongue dipped with exquisite tenderness into her mouth, finding her own willing tongue and moving sinuously against it.

It was the softest, sweetest kiss that Claudia had ever experienced, but that didn't make it any less erotic. Marco was taking it so slowly that she was acutely aware of every tiny movement of his lips, every nuance in the way his tongue stroked hers. The effect on the rest of her body was incredible. She was trembling all over and her heart was racing. Every nerve ending in her body was tingling and desire was pulsing deep within her.

Her eyes were still closed and there was no contact between them apart from the ongoing kiss and his hands cradling her face. But she could feel the heat radiating off his powerful body and she needed to touch him. She lifted her hands and pressed her palms against his chest.

A shiver of delight ran through her as she felt his skin, hot and wet, under her hands. Then, she let her hands glide around his ribcage and slip up between his shoulder blades, so that he was encircled in her arms.

A tiny step forward and she pressed herself against him, revelling in the feel of his hard, almost naked body next to hers.

Suddenly he pulled back from the kiss. Her eyes flew open and a small sound of protest escaped her. Marco was looking at her intently and there was a slight crease between his black eyebrows. His mouth was open a fraction and she watched, almost mesmerized, as he ran his tongue over his lower lip.

Then he turned and opened the shower door. A blast of cool air passed over her, making her shiver, as Marco stepped out and reached for a towel.

Ten minutes later Claudia opened the bathroom door carefully and peeked out. Luckily Marco was nowhere in sight, although she could hear his voice coming from the living area at the other end of the cottage as he talked to someone on his mobile phone.

She clutched a towel tightly around herself and dashed up to the safety of the bedroom, where she quickly dressed in some dry clothes from her bag. Then she sat on the bed and thought about what had happened.

Her body was still humming in reaction to his kiss. She had not intended it to happen—but it had been wonderful. For a few minutes she had forgotten all her worries and been carried away on a wave of happiness. It was as if she had gone back in time, and she and Marco were still together.

Suddenly an intense feeling of sadness washed over her. She shivered and hugged herself. What she'd thought she'd had with Marco had not been real. She could never get it back, because it had never truly existed in the first place. If Marco had cared for her at all, he could never have treated her so heartlessly.

She still didn't really know why he had followed her to Wales. Deep down inside, she longed to believe that he had realised that she meant something to him after all. In the shower he'd told her that he'd missed her, and maybe that meant something.

But it had been so hard to get over losing him—a large part of her was too frightened to even hope for anything ever again. It was safer to tell herself it could never happen.

Suddenly, her mobile phone started ringing.

'Claudia, darling,' Francesca said. 'I'm calling with the arrangements for the wedding. Do you have a notepad handy?'

A cold, heavy feeling sank in Claudia's stomach and she pulled a pen and notepad out of her bag.

She had more important things to worry about than her broken heart. In a few days time she had to marry Primo Vasile. She was already losing her father to his illness—she would not let Vasile send him to prison. She couldn't lose him any sooner than she had to.

Marco slipped his phone back into his pocket and smiled grimly. His legal team in Turin had finished securing all the necessary documents that proved the embezzlement of huge amounts of money from the Hazelton-Vasile pension fund. The evidence they'd obtained was substantial—more than enough to provide a watertight case against the perpetrators of the crime.

Everything was falling into place nicely. Within the next few days all Marco's old enemies would be completely obliterated.

The unmistakable sound of another mobile phone ringing upstairs drew him out of his thoughts. He realised that it must be Claudia's phone and walked to the doorway of the living room, wondering who was calling her.

Suddenly he was hit by a powerful memory of the night he'd left Claudia—the night he had discovered she'd betrayed him.

He stared blindly up the stairs, remembering the last day they'd spent together, here at this very cottage in Wales. He'd enjoyed her company so much, had felt so moved by the way she had opened up to him that the blow of her betrayal had been even harder to take.

It was shocking to think that she'd been prepared to delve so deep into her childhood memories to create such a convincing smokescreen. She'd talked about her mother, who had died when she was so young, and about her beloved grandmother with such feeling. It was repellent to realise that she'd simply been utilising her personal memories to dupe Marco.

Then another thought occurred to him with a sickening jolt and suddenly he knew the reason why she'd had to go back to her early childhood memories.

Twelve years ago Primo Vasile, with Francesca Hazelton's help, had viciously destroyed Marco's family. They'd taken everything that was precious from Marco and his innocent younger sister, Bianca—including the family home. Just days after the De Luca family business crumbled, Claudia's family had moved on to the De Luca estate. Her father, although he had not been directly involved with the takeover, was Vasile's business partner—and her stepmother was Vasile's partner in crime.

So Claudia had not been able to discuss her teenage years with Marco because, when she was thirteen years old, she had gone to live in the home that Vasile had cheated Marco's family out of.

Marco had always known that they shared this link—but, at the time of their relationship, he had genuinely believed she was unaware of it. He had been eighteen when his family had been destroyed and he had made it his business to know who was to blame. Claudia had been a child at the time and there was no reason for her to be aware of the family who had lived in her home before.

But now, thinking about the way she had focused all her childhood tales on her earlier years, he realised it was yet another way she had duped him.

A creak from above caught his attention and he looked up to see Claudia making her way down the wooden staircase.

He forced the memories to the back of his mind and studied her. She had changed into fresh clothes—a bulky jumper that did nothing to show off her feminine shape and dull, loose-fitting trousers. It didn't matter to him—in his mind's eye he could still see her in soaking wet, skin-tight jeans that clung to every intimate curve and a transparent T-shirt that showed her nipples jutting towards him in red-hot invitation.

He lifted his gaze to her face as she walked down to him and, as their eyes met, a crackle of tension passed between them. Her step faltered and she took a breath, as if she was gathering herself to speak. One glance at her body language and Marco knew that things were about to get interesting.

A buzz of anticipation ran through him and he realised he was looking forward to the exchange.

'I'd like you to leave now.'

Claudia's voice sounded clear and determined to her own ears, but her words had no effect on Marco. He continued to stand there, simply looking up at her with an intensity that made a shiver run down her spine. He was wearing fresh jeans and a luxurious midnight-blue sweater which hugged his body snugly and made her achingly aware of his superb athletic physique.

'I'm not ready to leave,' he replied. A powerful wave of energy was emanating from him and for some reason Claudia sensed danger. But his arrogant tone grated across her nerves and suddenly she was galvanised into action.

She walked down the stairs and slipped past him into the living room. As she went by him she couldn't help noticing that his black hair was nearly dry and was sexily dishevelled. It looked as if he'd simply rubbed it with a towel and pulled his fingers through it. Her own fingers suddenly tingled with the need to reach out and touch it, but she ignored the urge and made herself scan the room for his belongings.

'Here's your coat,' she said, picking up the leather jacket that he'd left lying across the back of the sofa. The leather was soft and supple in her hands and a tantalizing waft of his masculine scent filled her senses, but she ignored the disconcerting distraction and thrust the jacket towards him. 'Now, please just go.'

'Very polite,' Marco said, with an infuriating lift of his eyebrow as he caught hold of the jacket just in time to stop it falling to the floor. 'But, as I said, I'm not ready to go yet.'

'I don't care if you're ready.' Claudia was rapidly losing her temper. 'I didn't invite you to join me here. I didn't even tell you I was coming to Wales—you found that out by under-hand means. Is it surprising you're not welcome?'

'I was welcome enough in the shower,' Marco said, taking a step towards her.

'I told you to get out,' Claudia said, feeling her cheeks blaze as his eyes swept down across her body. Her clothes covered her well, but she knew he was remembering the many times he'd seen her naked.

'But you didn't mean it,' he said. 'In fact you soon made me feel very welcome indeed.'

'Well, you're not any more.' She spun round and marched to the front door of the cottage, which was in the far corner of the living room, and flung it open with a defiant flourish. Then she turned back to face him.

She gasped, startled to find him right behind her. He had followed her across the room as silently as the black cat she had imagined in the shower.

But, for once, his attention wasn't on her. He was staring out through the open door. Something in his expression made her turn round and follow his line of vision.

Her eyes opened wide with shock and it was her turn to stare.

A thick blanket of fog surrounded the cottage. And the rest of Wales, as far as she could see, which was only a few feet into the dense whiteness.

'That's incredible,' Marco said, stepping past her and walking a few paces into the fog. 'I've never seen anything like it.'

'Neither have I,' Claudia replied, momentarily forgetting her bad temper. The fog muffled their voices and the sound of his footsteps on the gravel as he walked further away into the thick white bank. 'I've seen fog rolling in off the sea—but that is extraordinary.'

She'd never seen fog so dense. In fact, she realised with a spike of alarm, Marco was starting to disappear from view.

'Come back!' she exclaimed. 'You'll get lost.'

'I can't even see my car,' he said, turning to walk back to her. The light from the doorway was bouncing back off the white wall of suspended moisture, making an eerie glow around him. 'I know it's only a few feet away.'

'You can't drive in this,' she said. It was impossible to see anything. The fog was too dense, and the light shining from the house didn't help at all. In fact the fog seemed to be acting like a mirror, reflecting the light straight back at them.

'Are you asking me to stay the night in the cottage?' he questioned. Even in the strange white glow she could see the gleam in his eye. 'With you.'

'No,' she said. 'I said you can't drive. But there's nothing to stop you sleeping in your car.'

She turned and walked back inside, but she didn't pull the door shut behind her. A moment later she heard Marco follow her in.

The clunk as he closed the door reverberated through her like an omen. Fogbound in the tiny cottage with Marco, she knew she was in for a long night.

CHAPTER FOUR

CLAUDIA took a deep breath and walked purposefully through to the bathroom. She didn't want to talk to Marco. Maybe, if she looked busy, he'd leave her alone.

She picked up the digital camera, which was lying on the floor near the door, gathered her wet clothes together and carried them through to the washing machine in the kitchen. Then she collected her laptop computer case from the bedroom and sat down at the kitchen table, looking at the camera.

Despite the battering it had taken at the beach, it didn't look to be in too bad shape. At the very least, she hoped the memory card would have survived—then she could transfer her photos on to the laptop and get on with writing her review.

At that moment it seemed much easier to focus on her job than to think about the night ahead.

'I need a drink.' Marco's voice right behind her made her jump. She wished he'd stop doing his cat impersonation, stalking silently round the cottage. 'And something to eat—I suddenly feel ravenous.'

The word *ravenous*, spoken in his sexy Italian accent, rumbled down her spine like thunder. She tried to suppress a shiver and spoke without looking up.

'I haven't got much food—I didn't plan on entertaining.'

'I'm not asking you to cook for me,' he replied, unaffected by her sharp tone. 'I knew I'd be staying the night, so I brought a few supplies myself. You can share them, if you'd like.'

'No, thank you,' she said crisply, irritated by his confident assumption that he would end up staying. If it wasn't for the fog, he would already be on his way. 'I've got work to do. Actually, if you're going to be cooking, I think I'll take myself into the other room.'

Still without looking at him, she picked up her stuff and headed through to the living room. The coffee table would be just as easy to work on, and at least Marco would be out of the way for a while. She knew it wouldn't take him all evening to cook and eat his supper. But she didn't let herself think about the long hours that stretched out before her.

She was surprised to notice a fire burning merrily in the hearth. She frowned, wondering when Marco had found the time to light it. It was burning so well that it must have been lit for a while. She hadn't noticed it when she came downstairs, but then she'd been concentrating hard on making Marco leave the cottage.

She sat down on the sofa, disconcerted to find that being around Marco still had the power to make her oblivious to her surroundings. When he looked at her, locking his rich espresso eyes with hers, it was as if the rest of the world ceased to exist.

It had always been like that. But, four years ago, Marco had exuded an all-encompassing charm that had wrapped around her like a gossamer blanket, shutting out all of her worries and melting her heart. She closed her eyes and pictured his face as it was then, back when they were lovers—the crinkles around his eyes as he laughed and his wide generous smile.

Now, when he looked at her, she was no longer transported away from her concerns. Instead, she felt a wave of anxiety rising within her. He had treated her so badly that she knew she could never let herself trust him again. But he still had the power to make her yearn to be with him.

She shook her head, trying to clear her troubling thoughts, and busied herself with her camera. She was pleased to discover the memory card was all right and loaded the photos on to the computer. She began to scroll through them, feeling increasingly hungry as the delicious smell of cooking drifted in from the kitchen.

'I thought you might change your mind,' Marco said, placing a glass of mulled wine and a plate of grilled cheese and tomato on toast on the coffee table beside her.

Right on cue, her stomach growled, making it impossible for her to refuse the food without looking churlish.

'Thank you,' she said briefly. She pulled the plate towards her, wondering if Marco had remembered that grilled cheese and tomato was one of her favourite light meals. It seemed a coincidence, but cheese and bread were easy foods to transport.

She picked up her glass and took a sip of aromatic mulled wine. The spicy liquid slipped down her throat easily, creating a delicious glow inside her.

They started to eat in silence, and Claudia found herself watching the orange flames flickering in the hearth as a way to avoid thinking about conversation. But as the minutes went by, she found herself becoming more relaxed in Marco's company. She didn't know if it was the warm mulled wine or the good food that helped to ease the tension, but by the time she finished the meal she felt a lot better.

'That was delicious—much tastier than the sandwich I

was planning,' Claudia said, breaking the silence. 'You made it seem so easy, and you got the fire started too.'

'It wasn't hard,' Marco replied. He slipped off the sofa for a moment to prod the fire with the poker, making a shower of glowing sparks fly upwards. Then, once he'd arranged the burning logs to his liking, he sat down again and turned to look at her, his dark eyes glinting in the firelight. 'It wasn't exactly a three course meal.'

'All the same, I probably would have burnt it.' Claudia smiled, feeling slightly surprised that they seemed to be having a normal conversation.

'I take it you still don't cook much,' Marco said. 'Don't you ever get tired of plain sandwiches and fruit?'

'Sometimes.' Claudia paused, taken aback that he remembered her tendency to live on simple uncooked food that took virtually no preparation. 'There never seems to be much point cooking for one.'

As soon as the words were out of her mouth she regretted it. It was silly to draw attention to the fact that she was on her own—Marco did not need to know that. And, now that she had agreed to get married, she soon wouldn't be on her own. But in her heart she knew she'd be more alone than ever.

'I may not cook much, but I do still enjoy baking. I took a cake into work for a colleague's birthday last week,' she rushed out, hoping to move the conversation on.

'One of your grandmother's recipes?' he asked.

'Yes.' She drew her brows together without realising what she was doing and frowned at him. Did he remember everything about her?

For some reason it bothered her. There were very few people who knew that her most treasured possession was her grandmother's handwritten recipe book. It was an ancient thing, with fragile curling grease-stained pages. But within its brown covers were wonderful recipes that represented more to Claudia that she could ever explain.

The lemon drizzle cake her grandma had made for Sunday tea when Claudia and her father, Hector, had escaped from Francesca for the afternoon. The large chocolate cake with expensive ingredients that meant it had only been made for birthdays. The cherry cake that Grandma said was Claudia's mother's favourite when she was a little girl. And Mother's Christmas Cake—which was Grandma's mother's recipe—Claudia's great-grandmother.

She'd never met her great grandmother and she'd lost her own mother when she was very young. But somehow that recipe book made her feel close to them. When she made those recipes she as if like she was making a connection to the past—as if she hadn't really lost them for ever.

'I'll get us a refill,' Marco said, reaching forward to take the empty wineglass from Claudia's hand. 'And I'll warm up some mince pies for dessert.'

Claudia leant back on the sofa, thinking how wonderful it was to be waited on. For such a dynamic, successful man, Marco was really very skilled in the kitchen and was not too proud to get down to work preparing food.

One of the reasons Claudia never cooked was that she didn't really know how to make even the most basic of meals. Her grandmother had taught her to bake cakes, but her stepmother, Francesca, had no interest in cooking and didn't see it as a useful skill. As far as she was concerned, you employed a chef or always ate out.

She heard a muted clang as Marco closed the oven door and

for some reason Claudia found herself thinking about the many times his sister, Bianca, had sung his praises. There was no doubt that Marco had taken his role as his sister's guardian very seriously, even to the point of preparing meals for her himself.

She looked over her shoulder and saw him coming back into the room with two refilled wineglasses in his hands.

'Bianca often told me how wonderfully you took care of her after the death of both your parents,' Claudia said. 'Is that when you learnt to cook?'

A nasty jolt jarred through Marco at Claudia's comment.

She had no business talking about Bianca as if they were friends—not after the things she'd done. Also, hearing her mention his mother—the De Luca family's shameful betrayer—was unacceptable.

'My mother is not dead,' Marco said shortly, holding the fierce rush of anger that powered through him in check. 'I don't know where she is now, and I do not care to know. She betrayed our family and abandoned Bianca, her only daughter, when she was still a child.'

'I'm so sorry.' Claudia looked genuinely upset and confused as she pushed her hair back from her face with a shaky movement of her hand. Her eyes were wide with concern. 'What happened?'

'I looked after my sister, of course,' Marco said, staring down at her coldly.

He knew that wasn't the answer she was looking for, but there was no way he was going to discuss how Primo Vasile had seduced his mother, tempting her into her treachery against his father.

Although treachery was something that Claudia could

understand—just like his mother, she had committed the same crime. But he wasn't ready to accuse her of that now.

'I'm sorry. I didn't know,' Claudia said quietly. 'About your mother, I mean. I always got the impression she had died at the same time as your father.'

'As far as I am concerned, she did,' Marco said flatly.

Claudia looked at his stony face in silence. It must have been awful for Bianca to lose her mother like that—worse, in many ways, than if she had actually died. No wonder they never talked about her.

'Thank goodness, for Bianca's sake, that she had such a devoted brother to look after her,' Claudia said.

For a long moment Marco was silent, staring into the crackling fire with dark eyes. She began to think that she'd made him really angry by bringing up a sore subject from his past. But then he seemed to shake off his black mood and turned back to her again.

'I never *learnt* to cook—it always seemed instinctive,' he said, finally sitting down on the sofa beside her.

'Well, I guess I don't have the right instincts,' she said wryly, pleased that he was talking to her again. 'Everything I try to cook comes out tough and overdone, or raw on the inside and burnt on the outside.'

'You can bake cakes,' Marco said. 'But I think photography is where your true instincts lie. I'd love to see the photos you took this afternoon.'

'Really?' Claudia glanced at him, suddenly feeling shy. She wasn't entirely sure she wanted him looking through her photos. But there were still a lot of hours of the evening to get through and she should make the most of the quiet mood they seemed to have reached.

'I'll get some mince pies,' Marco said. 'Then we'll look at them together.'

It didn't take him long to return with a plate of spicily fragrant mince pies, then she started scrolling through the beach photos. She was apprehensive to be looking at them for the first time in front of Marco, but at the same time very pleased with what she had achieved that afternoon.

'They're amazing,' Marco said, moving closer to her and angling the laptop screen for his benefit. A moment later his hand covered hers as he took control of the computer, moving through the photographs at a rate that suited him.

A *frisson* passed through her as his fingers brushed hers, but she pulled her hand away carefully, trying not to let him notice the way that even that slight physical contact had affected her.

'These pictures are really incredible,' Marco said. Somehow he had manoeuvred the computer on the coffee table so that it was completely in front of him. 'The way you've caught the surging elemental energy is amazing. I can all but feel the press of the brooding sky and hear the roar of the waves.'

Claudia stared at him, startled by his praise.

'Do you mind if I scroll back through some of your other photos?' he asked, already starting to scan back through her files.

The images flipped by, going backwards in time. December in a London park. Bonfire night fireworks in November. Autumn trees in the English countryside. The grape harvest in Piedmont with the Alps in the background.

It might have seemed as if those pictures represented her life over the last few months. But they were just places she'd been—photos she'd taken for work. They did nothing to convey the distress that had been growing inside her after her father had been taken seriously ill.

Suddenly she noticed she was watching images of the family home and vineyard near Turin flash past. They were personal photos and she should stop Marco looking at them. But then, at that moment, she found herself looking at a photo of her father.

He was sitting in the courtyard by the fountain pool and he was smiling and looking happy. Not as robust as in his younger years—but there were no real signs of the illness that was about to strike him. He appeared cheerful and well—not the frail shadow of himself he had been in recent months since he had become so ill.

She stared at the image, wishing herself back in time. Wishing her father still looked happy and fit. But that was never going to happen. He was never going to recover from his illness.

All she could do was watch him fade away. And marry a man she detested. That way her father would not have to lose everything and face a criminal investigation, when it was almost more than he could do to simply hang on to the last fragile threads of his life.

Her vision blurred and her eyes were full of tears. There was nothing she could do to stop them, so she squeezed her eyelids closed and turned away, trying to think about something different.

Marco was looking at images of his old family home. Distinctly uneasy emotions were rumbling within him as he studied the pictures of the house and surrounding vineyards.

He wasn't seeing the elderly man in the foreground of the photo, although he'd recognised Hector Hazelton at once. He was staring at the fountain courtyard, remembering all the afternoons he'd spent there with his much younger sister, taking time to play with her before going off to meet his friends.

A sudden burst of fury exploded in him and he felt his hands clench involuntarily into fists. That property should still belong to his family. His sister Bianca should have finished growing up there, with a loving mother and father— but instead Claudia had grown up in his rightful home with her father, Hector, and with that witch Francesca Hazelton.

It was twelve years since the De Luca family had been destroyed, but the fury that had consumed Marco then continued to rage through him. His family had been torn apart from within—had suffered the ultimate treachery. Betrayed by one of their own—Marco's mother.

It had started when Francesca Hazelton insinuated herself into his mother's life, pretending to be her friend and gaining her trust. Then she had introduced her cousin, Primo Vasile.

It hadn't taken long for the serpent, Vasile, to use his snake-like charm to seduce Marco's mother. Afterwards, he had lured her into turning against her own family. She'd taken a vast amount of money from Marco's father and revealed crucial business secrets that had enabled Vasile to bring the family business down. He'd taken whatever he'd wanted and destroyed everything else.

Marco's father had been weak, blind to his wife's treachery. He had not struck out against her when he had the chance, when he'd first discovered her duplicity. Marco would not make the same mistake.

Now he knew that Claudia was a snake in the grass, and he would not fail to treat her in the way that she deserved. She would pay for everything she had done—to him and to his sister.

Suddenly, despite the vengeful thoughts that filled his mind, Marco felt a change come over Claudia. She'd been sitting quietly beside him, making no comment as he looked through her photographs, but he realised that she must have seen his temper flare just now.

With a supreme effort of will, Marco consciously forced his body to relax and removed signs of his anger from his expression. The need for revenge burned stronger than ever within him, but he had to lock it away inside for a short while longer.

He turned and looked at Claudia.

What he saw doused his fury as effectively as a bucket of cold water.

Claudia was sitting with her eyes squeezed shut, huge tears rolling down her ashen face. She looked so sad and vulnerable that Marco reacted instinctively to her distress, momentarily forgetting what she had done to him and Bianca.

He slid off the sofa and kneeled in front of her, the anger that had overtaken him a moment before completely gone.

'Claudia.'

He saw her shoulders stiffen as his voice penetrated her misery, then she opened her eyes to look at him.

'Sorry,' she mumbled, rubbing the flats of her hands self-consciously across her face and blinking to clear her eyes. 'I didn't mean to cry. It was just that the photo of my father got to me.'

'Don't apologise,' Marco said, catching her hands with his. 'I didn't realise looking at those photos would upset you.'

'You weren't to know that my father is ill.' She smiled at him weakly, but he could tell she had a tenuous grip on her emotions and was only just holding back the flow of tears.

'Is he very ill?' Marco asked softly.

Claudia nodded, biting her lower lip as if to stop it quivering. 'He won't get better—there's no hope of that. It's just a matter of time.'

'I'm sorry,' he said, lifting one hand to cradle her cheek gently. She might be a consummate actress, who had wheedled her way dishonestly into Bianca's life and then into his. But that did not mean she wasn't capable of loving her father—and her distress looked genuine.

Hearing Marco's voice so deep with sympathy and feeling the tenderness of his touch was suddenly too much for Claudia. She burst into fresh tears and buried her face in her hands, wishing she could shut out the misery that overwhelmed her when she thought about her father.

A second later she felt Marco's arms close around her. He was strong and warm and she found herself clinging to him, sobbing in earnest.

'I want to go and visit him,' she wept. 'But I'm scared of how much worse he'll be since I saw him only last week. I'm not strong enough to hide how I'm feeling, but I can't let him see me like this—it wouldn't be fair to upset him.'

'It will be all right, *dolce mia.* I'll take you to see your father tomorrow,' Marco murmured against her hair. 'And you *will* be strong when you need to be. But it doesn't matter if he sees you're upset—it shows how much you care.'

She clung to him, thinking how much like the old Marco he suddenly seemed. Part of her didn't want to accept comfort from him—not after everything that had happened between them. But another part wanted to believe that the man she had fallen in love with four years ago was still there. That man would have comforted her. That man would have moved heaven and earth if it made her feel better.

'He doesn't know he's dying.' Claudia heard the strangled tones of her own voice, but now she had started confiding in Marco she couldn't stop. It was such an overwhelming relief to share the awful burden. 'My stepmother and his doctors thought it was best to keep it from him. If he gets upset his heart couldn't take it.'

'Don't you think he deserves to know?' Marco sounded shocked. The thought flashed through Claudia's mind that Marco would never forgive anyone for keeping such news from him. But then she couldn't imagine Marco ever being frail enough to warrant such considerations.

'I don't know,' she replied, feeling utterly helpless. 'My stepmother told me it would kill him to find out.'

The idea that Marco might disapprove of her actions suddenly made her feel cold and bleak, undermining the grip she had been slowly regaining on her emotions. She burst into renewed tears and hung her head miserably.

'I apologise. It wasn't my place to say that. I don't know the whole situation,' Marco said, pulling her close to him once again. 'We'll talk to his doctors. Maybe his condition has stabilised.'

'Thank you.' Claudia pressed her face against the soft merino wool of his sweater, feeling the reassuring strength and warmth of his body radiating through the garment. 'That would be wonderful. I couldn't seem to make the doctors talk to me properly—I think my stepmother told them I didn't understand Italian well enough.'

'Where is he?' Marco asked.

'In a hospital in Turin,' she replied.

'Is your stepmother there with him?'

'I don't know. I doubt it,' Claudia said, resting with her face against his shoulder and her hand flat against his chest. His arms were wrapped around her and at that moment she felt totally safe, cocooned in his embrace. 'Francesca divides her time between London and Turin, but even when she's in Italy she doesn't visit him much, even though she has an apartment in the city. She never liked the countryside—she won't go to the Piedmont house unless she has to.'

She spoke sadly, wishing that her father could have fallen in love with someone who cared for him more than her stepmother did, when suddenly she felt an almost imperceptible ripple of tension pass through Marco. She pulled away from him slightly, sitting upright so that she could look into his face. The hardness in his eyes startled her, making her heart skip a beat.

'What's wrong?' she asked, wondering if he disapproved of Francesca's lack of devotion. Or maybe he was judging *her* for not dropping everything to remain at her father's bedside.

'Nothing.' He softened his expression at once. But his blood was boiling at the discovery that Francesca Hazelton didn't even like the country estate she had taken from his family and moved into only days after his father had died. 'I was just thinking how hard it must have been on you, being tied to London by your work when really you just wanted to be in Italy with your father.'

'I would have given up my job in an instant,' she said, 'but my father wouldn't let me. I was furious with Francesca for telling him my plan to quit work, but he got so upset at the idea of me putting my life on hold while he was ill that I simply couldn't go against his wishes. I've flown back to Turin almost every weekend.'

'No wonder you look tired,' Marco said, lifting his hand and sliding it through her hair to cup the side of her head.

'I must look a state,' Claudia gasped, all of a sudden feeling awkward about how she had let herself weep with such un-dignified abandon. 'My face must be blotchy and I can't bear to imagine how red my eyes are.'

'There are no blotches.' Marco raised his other hand so that he was holding her head on both sides, his fingers buried deep in her hair. 'And your eyes are not red—they are simply luminous, glowing with the emotion you feel inside.'

'You're just saying that to make me feel better.' She smiled, knowing he must be lying. But it was a kind lie and his words had lifted her spirits.

'You look beautiful,' he said, gazing at her in a way that suddenly made her heart beat faster. He was still holding her head captive in his gentle hands, and he began to pull her slowly towards him.

She gazed at him, thinking he seemed more devastatingly good looking than ever. The firelight was casting a gorgeous glow over his face, his dark eyes were glinting with reflected amber lights and his black hair was gilded with gold.

He was going to kiss her—she knew it with absolute cer-tainty. But then he paused, letting his mouth hover only a fraction away from hers.

At the back of her mind the voice of reason cried out for her to take this chance to back away from him. She knew she shouldn't get involved with him again. Nothing had changed—he was still the man who had discarded her without a backwards glance. The man who had broken her heart.

She drew in a long shuddering breath and closed her eyes, struggling with her inner turmoil.

Her lips were tingling in expectation of his kiss and her whole body was quivering with the desire that was rising within her, but she knew she shouldn't give in to it. In a few days time she had to travel to the Caribbean to marry Primo Vasile. That was the hard reality of her life.

Her idyllic time with Marco was a distant memory. It had happened—but it wasn't real. Not in the way that she remembered it. She had fallen in love with him but although he might have enjoyed spending time with her for a while, it was obvious that he had not felt the same way.

Now he was back in her life and he seemed very different—harder, angrier. She'd never intended to turn to him for comfort over her father. But after the stresses of the last couple of days, looking at the photograph had really got to her. And, although she'd tried, she hadn't been able to hold back her tears. But just because he had offered her sympathy over her father's illness did not mean that she had to fall into his arms.

'I can't do this.' Her voice was small, but resolute. She sat up straighter and tried to pull away from him.

'Yes, you can,' he said. 'You want this as much as I do.'

A moment later Marco's mouth closed over hers.

CHAPTER FIVE

CLAUDIA clung to Marco, giving herself over to his kiss completely. She wanted to lose herself in his arms for a few blissful minutes and forget all the worries that had been weighing so heavily on her. There was no going back now—she didn't want to go back. She couldn't let herself think about what she was doing—that might give her rational mind time to protest.

'I'm going to make you mine again.'

His voice was unbearably sexy—dark and chocolaty, it rippled through her flesh like a physical sensation, making her yearn for him even more.

His hands slipped under her top and moved across her back, his fingers spread wide and his palms hot and smooth against her skin. A deeply expressive sigh escaped her as she felt him caressing her. But she needed more. She needed to feel his naked skin under her fingertips.

It was as if he had read her mind, because he quickly stripped off his sweater.

'You feel so good,' she murmured, running her hands up his sides and across his ribs to his chest. She felt his pectoral muscles flex under her fingers and his nipples tighten into small hard points.

Then, Marco took hold of her waist and a split second later they were both standing. The open fire was warm beside her and she couldn't help running her eyes over his half naked body.

The golden light flickered on his bronzed skin, highlighting the well-defined muscles of his athletic physique and making the fine tangle of black hair on his chest seem more powerfully masculine than ever. Her stomach fluttered with anticipation and she felt a warm wave of desire rolling over her body.

Suddenly the sound of Claudia's mobile phone ringing jarred through the air.

Marco stiffened, feeling the mood shatter. He turned away and picked up the intrusive item from the coffee table.

He glanced at the caller display and another jolt stabbed through him.

Primo Vasile.

He handed Claudia the phone and walked out of the room.

Marco stood in front of the sink and splashed cold water on to his face. Powerful emotions had surged around his body, taking him completely by surprise. But now he was determined to regain control.

He'd followed Claudia to Wales with the ruthless intention of bedding her out of revenge.

They'd made love many times in the past—but every time she'd laid in his arms she had been deceiving him. That knowledge was unbearable.

Marco had instinctively known the only way he could expunge the anger that gripped him when he realised how he'd been duped was to turn the tables on her. He would take her to bed on his own terms, for his own satisfaction—and then he would discard her.

He hadn't been prepared for how badly he still wanted her. His desire for her had burned through his veins like wildfire—consuming every rational thought in his head.

Then, when Claudia's mobile phone had rung and he'd seen that it was Primo Vasile, an overwhelming surge of possessiveness had stormed through him. He hated Vasile and was determined to thwart his plans in any way he could. But once again he had been shocked by the strength of his feeling towards Claudia.

He gritted his teeth and opened the bathroom door. He would control his emotions—just like he always had. And, when he had bedded Claudia one last time, she'd be out of his system. Then he would cast her aside.

Claudia sat on the sofa, looking into the fire. Her body was buzzing with unfulfilled desire, but she kept telling herself she'd had a lucky escape. She hadn't answered the phone call—she'd been too lost in the moment with Marco to bear to talk to Primo Vasile—but it had given her a chance to get a hold of herself.

She stood up and walked across the room in agitation. What was wrong with her? Why would she even think of letting Marco make love to her?

He'd broken her heart and there was no reason to assume he would treat her any differently if she got involved with him again. Except, a little voice inside her said, apart from the terrible way he'd finished their relationship, he'd always treated her with incredible respect and tenderness.

But it didn't matter anyway—because, even if she wanted to be with Marco again, she couldn't.

Suddenly a heavy band of panic wrapped around her, constricting her throat, making it hard to breathe. She'd had no choice when she'd agreed to marry Primo, but she clung desperately to the fact that it was to be a marriage in name only. Later, after her father could no longer be hurt, she would leave him.

Suddenly tears welled up in her eyes and she knew she was about to burst into tears. It was awful—truly awful—to have to think about her escape from Primo at the same time as thinking about her father's death.

She blinked desperately, determined not to let Marco see her cry again. That was what had made things so complicated in the first place. She didn't want to talk about her father's illness any more—she couldn't bear it. And she also knew that if she got upset again she might end up telling Marco everything—about her stepmother and Vasile blackmailing her. That was the last thing she wanted.

Deep down inside she knew that someone as self assured and strong as Marco would never understand what she was doing for her father. He'd be convinced there must be another way to save him. He was used to being in control of his life and he had power and money.

But Claudia had no power. And the only way to get money was to marry and release her trust fund. There was nothing she could do to change that, without causing great distress to her father on his deathbed. And she would never, ever do that.

She turned and paced across the room, determined to think about something else. She went to the window and pressed her nose to the glass, cupped her hands round her face to block out the light from the lamp and stared out into the night.

Then a sound from behind her made her turn round.

'Come and join me,' Marco said, setting down two fresh glasses of wine on the coffee table.

'I was looking at the fog,' she said, reluctant to sit with him. As soon as she'd laid eyes on him, her earlier feelings of attraction had started to resurface. 'It's still so thick you can't see a thing.'

Marco crossed the room and joined her at the window. He had not put his sweater back on and she couldn't take her eyes off him. His movements were fluid and athletic, but everything about his stance made her think about the sheer strength contained within his powerful masculine form.

'It's as if the rest of the world doesn't exist,' Marco said. 'The cottage is completely cut off. For a city dweller, that's a strange feeling.'

As soon as he'd said the words a shiver ran through her. It truly was as if the rest of the world didn't exist.

Then, to make matters worse, he lifted both hands to gently cradle her head, letting his fingers slip between the silky tresses of her hair. A whisper of electric desire tingled between them, but Claudia felt herself tense and she tried to step away.

'It's…it's just that my life is so complicated,' Claudia stammered. 'I can't do this…I mean I can't get involved with you again.'

'Everyone's life is complicated,' Marco said. 'But there's one simple fact that matters right now—tonight we are here, alone, unable to leave even if we wanted to.'

Claudia lifted her face to meet his gaze and, as she looked into his eyes, the familiar feeling that she was the only woman in the world came over her. And in a way that was true. Cut off from everything by the thick fog, they were alone. He was the only man, and she was the only woman.

CHAPTER SIX

MARCO stood by the window, watching Claudia walk away from him. Even dressed in her shapeless garments she still looked as hot as hell. When she bent down to pick up her glass of wine, a renewed blast of desire fired through his body.

He wanted her badly.

He frowned, his eyes following her as she walked over to the fireplace and started looking at the Christmas ornaments that had been arranged on the mantelpiece.

'I can't believe it,' she said suddenly. She picked up a couple of little figures and carried them across the room to show him. 'My grandmother had these exact same ornaments!'

Marco watched her walking towards him, captivated by the bewitching sway of her hips and the gentle bounce of her full breasts beneath the wool of her sweater as she moved.

'I suppose it's not so much of a coincidence really,' Claudia was saying. 'I guess Grandma and Gwen went shopping at the same local craft fairs.'

'They're interesting pieces,' Marco said, forcing his raging libido under control. 'I haven't seen anything like them before. Do you think they were made locally?'

'Probably,' Claudia said, holding the figures in her cupped

hands next to her breast, in a totally natural gesture of happy affection. 'Oh, they remind me of my Grandma. And her decoration box.'

A strange feeling tightened inside Marco as he looked at her. He'd heard her talk about her grandmother before. But, now that he knew what kind of person Claudia was, it was strangely discomfiting to hear her talk with such animation about her past.

'Tell me about the box,' Marco said, interested in spite of the voice inside his head telling him he didn't need to hear any more of her childhood tales.

'There's nothing much to tell,' she said. 'It contained the tree ornaments that Grandma had collected over the years. She had a different story to tell about each one.' She smiled, momentarily lost in her thoughts. 'I loved to imagine my own mother helping her to hang those decorations on the tree. And every year Grandma would buy just one more—usually from a local craft fair.'

'Did you help your grandmother to decorate?' Marco asked.

Claudia looked at him and hesitated, wondering whether she wanted to share any more personal memories with Marco. He seemed to have remembered every detail of every single thing she'd confided in him that summer four years ago.

She found her gaze fixed on his gorgeous face. He really was breathtakingly good-looking. And when he looked at her like that, giving her his undivided attention, it felt as if she was somehow more important than usual. He seemed genuinely engaged in what she had to say. And the very fact that he remembered what she'd told him so long ago was proof that he listened properly and was interested.

'My father and I used to visit her every year before Christmas and help her decorate,' she said, asking herself what harm could it do to tell him—he already knew so much about her.

'Your stepmother didn't join you?'

'She always said that Wales was much too far away from civilisation. And she was allergic to Grandma's dog,' Claudia replied, suddenly feeling indescribably glad that Francesca had never made her presence felt in her grandmother's home.

Up until that moment she'd always taken it for granted that her stepmother had wanted nothing to do with her real mother's home or family. But the sudden unpleasant thought that Francesca might easily have insisted on coming to Wales shook her. Would those childhood memories hold the same treasured place in her heart if Francesca had stamped them with her indelible mark?

'My stepmother didn't approve of Grandma's decorations or her taste in fairy lights,' Claudia said, unable to resist a little dig at Francesca. 'According to her rules, lights should be white. Or occasionally another single colour designed to blend in with her theme for Christmas.'

'So now you hate white lights?' Marco asked, his lips quirking with amusement.

'No, of course not. I suppose it's just that they remind me of the way my stepmother took over Christmas. Each year she'd have a new theme. Top designers would come in and decorate—I was never allowed to help. Everything was brand-new, and at the end of Christmas she'd just throw it all out.'

'So now you don't like new decorations either?' Marco said with a glint in his eye.

'I don't have anything against new decorations,' Claudia said, refusing to rise to his provocation. 'It's wonderful choosing a new tree ornament or garland for your home. But it's lovely to keep the old ones too. And each one has a memory of the Christmas when you first had it.'

She looked up at Marco and was startled to see his gaze was still locked on her. There was a strange expression in his eyes that she couldn't quite read, and suddenly she wished she hadn't been quite so open with her memories after all.

'What are you doing for Christmas?' she asked, saying the first thing that came into her mind.

Unfortunately, saying that suddenly reminded her that by Christmas she would be married to Vasile. A cold feeling settled in the pit of her stomach, but she turned to put the ornaments back in their place and tried to ignore it.

'I'm having a quiet Christmas this year,' Marco said shortly.

Something in his voice made Claudia think he found the question intrusive.

A flash of irritation sparked within her. How hypocritical of him to be happy prying into her life but resent it when she showed an interest in his. It was hardly a personal question.

'Will you spending it with Bianca?' she asked. 'I hope she's doing well for herself—you haven't told me anything about what she's up to these days.'

She felt a prickle of sadness over her lost friendship with Bianca—she was sure that Marco had something to do with his sister dropping her so completely. She wanted to say that she missed Bianca but she couldn't bring herself to say the words. It would sound too much like she had missed Marco.

'She's fine. She lives in America,' Marco said abruptly, striding across the room to throw another couple of logs on to the fire. 'That should do for a while,' he added, picking up the poker.

He'd moved so quickly and unexpectedly that Claudia felt a sudden gust of air pass across her skin, making the hairs on the back of her neck stand up. For a moment she was reminded of the raw energy of the natural elements—a raging sea or a torrential storm.

The energy that crackled off Marco was physical and entirely masculine. It suddenly made her think of making love.

'There's lots of wood in the basket.' There was a tremor in her voice and she didn't even try to tear her eyes away from Marco's exquisite physique as he prodded the logs, making the fire hiss and spark. 'There should be enough to last all evening.'

She watched him replacing the poker in the wrought iron stand, mesmerised by the sight of his muscles rippling beneath his bronzed skin as he moved. Her fingers itched to touch him but, as he stood up, she fled across the room to an armchair, never taking her eyes off his magnificent form.

He picked up his glass of wine. Then he sat down on the sofa and turned his gaze on to her.

As their eyes met, a bolt of electricity zinged between them. He'd seen the way she was looking at him, knew exactly what she was thinking

He turned the tables on her, letting his eyes draw a trail from the tips of her toes all the way up her body.

She shivered and drew her legs on to the chair, curling up as if it would protect her from his sexual gaze. But the truth was she didn't want protection. She wanted Marco to make love to her. She was here with him now, and for just one night she could shut out the rest of the world.

Marco looked at Claudia's long lean legs folded beneath her and felt his heart start to thud with desire. He thought about those supple limbs wrapped tight around his hips, urging him on as he thrust powerfully into her willing body, and suddenly he was as hard as iron.

A blast of anger ripped through him and he cursed himself for wanting her so badly.

He looked at her, curled seductively in the chair, watching him provocatively from beneath a curtain of long hair. The expression on her face told him that she was hot for him.

She lifted her chin slightly as a spark of awareness passed between them. Then she pushed her hair back over her shoulder and his eyes were drawn to the alluring lift of her breasts beneath her sweater.

'That top suits you,' he said, looking at the outline of her nipples beneath the soft material.

'Really? It's old and kind of shapeless—I think it's been washed too many times,' she said. She dropped her gaze and ran her hand over the sleeve, but he'd caught sight of a glimmer of pleasure in her eyes.

However, the sweater covered up far too much of her body for the way he was currently feeling. The open neck fell quite low on her slender form, showing the full length of her elegant neck and revealing part of her collar-bone. Suddenly it seemed like the sexiest thing he'd ever seen.

The beguiling way the exquisite shape of the bone disappeared under the wool drew his gaze like a magnet.

'You have a beautiful neck,' he said. 'And your collar-bone is divine.'

She turned to look at him, surprise flaring in her eyes and a pretty flush returning to her cheeks. But he knew she was pleased by his compliments.

'Let me see,' he said, demonstrating with a gesture how he wanted her to pull the sweater aside.

Her hand moved as if by instinct to mirror his, but she paused, her fingers resting against the base of her throat, and looked at him.

He met her gaze with his own, wondering if she was going to behave coyly. But then she tipped her head to one side and pulled the neckline of the sweater lower, revealing her finely structured collar-bone.

'It's delectable,' he murmured, hearing his own voice drop an octave as another surge of desire rushed through him. 'I want to run my tongue along it, then taste the hollow at the base of your throat and feel your pulse beating.'

He stood up and walked towards her, his heart pumping powerfully as he saw her throat move when she swallowed nervously. He took her hands with his and pulled her slowly to her feet.

Then, before she had chance to protest, he led her back across the room and pulled her down so that she was sitting astride him on the sofa. He was ready to make love to her—his desire burning through him like molten lava. It was all he could do to contain his rising sexual need—but he was going to take things slowly.

Another flash of surprise showed on her face as she found herself straddling him, but he slipped his arms around her quickly and leant forward to press his open mouth against her neck.

An uneven sigh escaped her and Marco knew that he had rediscovered one of her sensitive areas. She had always loved it when he'd nuzzled and kissed her neck.

He enjoyed it too—she was so responsive to him that he gained as much pleasure as he knew he was giving.

Her hands were gripping his shoulders and he felt her fingers tighten reflexively as he dipped his head lower and traced her collar-bone with his tongue. The skin was smooth and warm beneath his mouth and the small sounds of delight she was making stirred his senses even more.

He let his hands slip under the hem of the sweater and slowly slide up to cup her breasts.

A deep moan of appreciation escaped her and Marco closed his eyes for a second, lost in his own moment of satisfaction. It was too long since he'd felt the glorious weight of her breasts in his palms, too long since he'd massaged their softness with his hands.

He reached behind her to unhook her bra, then his hands moved back to her breasts. He lifted them slightly, adjusting the position of his hold so that he could close the forefinger and thumb of each hand around her nipples. He rolled them gently and felt a shot of sexual excitement power through him.

'Oh!' He heard the involuntary quaver of arousal resonate through Claudia's voice and an answering shudder of pure arousal shook him.

'I need to see you,' he said, releasing her breasts just long enough to pull the sweater up and over her head. He threw it aside impatiently with her bra, then paused, momentarily transfixed by the magnificent sight of her naked breasts.

Her creamy skin glowed in the flickering firelight and her breasts were full and perfectly shaped. They were rising and falling with the rapid rate of her breathing, making them even more alluring to him.

His gaze focused on her nipples and he felt his mouth watering with the need to close his lips around them and caress them with his tongue. They were pert and ready, jutting invitingly towards him.

He leant forward and took one hard pink nipple into his mouth.

Claudia moaned again, feeling her world start to dissolve into absolute bliss.

Wonderful sensations spiralled out from her breasts. Marco's mouth felt gloriously hot against her flesh and his expert tongue was teasing her nipple in a way that sent darts of pure sexual energy shooting through her. He held her other breast in his hand, massaging the nipple between his finger and thumb.

The pleasure he was giving to each breast combined within her, intensifying the rapturous response that consumed her whole body. She arched her back, letting her head fall backwards, and pushed her breasts towards him. Her entire body was glowing with rekindled desire and, deep down in her most feminine place, an insistent throbbing need was building.

Then Marco pulled back from her and she felt herself sway with the sudden loss of contact and sensual stimulation.

She opened her eyes and found herself gazing into the dark depths of his eyes. In the warm firelight they looked almost black, but maybe that was just pure arousal. She was breathing deeply and, with every breath, she was ultra-aware of her aching breasts rising and falling, straining almost of their own volition towards him.

She yearned to feel his mouth work its magic on her again, feel his hand caressing her. But he continued to hold her gaze. And with each passing moment she was more aware of her breasts, until they began to tingle and sing almost as if he was still touching her. Her breathing deepened further and suddenly she saw a smile flash across Marco's face.

'You are so sexy,' he said. 'And I'm going to take this slowly—take every ounce of pleasure.'

A flutter of excitement started inside her, but she didn't have time to think about his words because at that moment he leant forward and pressed his open mouth against her neck.

A mixture of ticklishness and breathless arousal skittered through her and once again she was overtaken by the intensity of feeling Marco was able to elicit from her so naturally. It seemed as if he was perfectly in tune with her body and knew exactly how to touch or caress her to give her extraordinary pleasure. And with every second that passed she was growing more and more aroused.

She wriggled on his lap, suddenly acutely aware of the fact that she was sitting astride him, that her most sensitive place was open to him if he chose to touch her.

Just the thought of his fingertips exploring that place made her heart rate accelerate and she shifted position again, the muscled strength of his legs hard under her thighs. She looked down and found herself staring at the shape of his erection pressing against the fabric of his jeans.

'Would you help me?' Marco's voice took her by surprise and, before she fully realised what he was doing, he had lifted her to one side, unfastened her trousers and pulled them off, taking her briefs at the same time. He stood up, discarding jeans and boxers in the process, and reached to a small packet. Then he sat back again and lifted her into her position astride his lap.

Claudia took the condom with shaking fingers and rolled it on to him. The feel of his hard masculine flesh beneath her hands set her body trembling afresh. She drew in an uneven breath, suddenly desperate to feel him moving inside her.

But instead of rolling her over onto her back on the sofa, Marco slid his hand between her legs, seeking out the place that had been longing for his touch only moments before.

Exquisite sensations flowed through her with every gentle stroke of his fingertips. She closed her eyes and let her head fall forward, surrendering to the pleasure he was giving her. Then he started to increase the pressure and tempo of his touch, and wave after wave of fire burned through her veins, setting her nerve-endings alight so that it felt as if her whole body was shimmering with delight.

She heard her own breath coming in faster and faster gasps. Then she was panting, small moaning sounds escaping every time she exhaled. She began to writhe on Marco's lap, unable to contain the extraordinary feelings that were continuing to grow.

The whole wonderful experience was building, like a mighty crescendo rising within her, swelling to fill her entire awareness. Then, suddenly, her climax crashed over her and unstoppable waves of blissful sensation rolled through her.

'Marco! Marco!' she cried, trembling uncontrollably. She gasped for breath, soaring through the heights of all-consuming pleasure.

His arms were round her, holding her shaking body, supporting her as she slowly started to drift back to earth. Then, suddenly, before the sublime rapture of her orgasm had faded, his hands slid to her waist and he lifted her up, holding her so that she was poised above him, his hard erection pressing ready against her pulsing flesh.

Claudia's eyes flew open as she registered her new position, her body already reacting to the new stimulation, the promise of more bliss to come.

Marco's gaze was fixed on her face and she knew he was watching her, sharing in the experience of her climax. And now he was about to take her back to those unsurpassed heights.

She gasped as he pulled down on her hips, guiding her so that his hard masculine length slid smoothly into place.

A renewed surge of excitement shook her body. And, as she felt him inside her, somehow everything seemed different, somehow even more amazing than before.

Her knees were on either side of him, supporting her weight, and she lifted and then lowered herself back down, feeling him sliding intimately within her body. She repeated the movement, rolling her hips to increase the friction between them, and she heard a low rumble of pleasure come from Marco.

Her own body was rapidly responding to the new stimulation and she found herself shaking. Her movements were becoming uneven, as every wave of pleasure crashing through her seemed to weaken her leg muscles.

Suddenly Marco took hold of her waist and pulled her tightly to him. Then, holding her close so that they were still joined, he lifted her and rolled them over so that she was lying on her back.

Claudia moaned out loud as her body sank back into the sofa, her legs wrapped around Marco. For a moment he lay still, his male hardness bedded deep within her. Her inner muscles clenched, as if she wanted to hold on to that moment, to him, for as long as possible.

Then he started to move, thrusting into her again and again. And every powerful thrust sent magnificent feelings surging through her. Once again she felt herself building towards a climax. Marco was an incredible lover and she was in thrall to his mastery of her body. Every move he made carried her higher and higher.

Then, suddenly, wonderfully, she pushed through the clouds into the heavens. Another orgasm, stronger and more intense than the first, took hold of her, carrying her away into a world of overwhelming fulfilment.

A moment later Marco arched up above her, a triumphant cry coming from deep within him as he gave a mighty shudder and reached his own powerful release.

He collapsed on top of her, his weight partially supported by his elbows, and she wrapped her arms tightly around him, enjoying her slow descent back to earth. She could feel his heart beating strongly beneath his ribs and for an instant she couldn't distinguish between his heartbeat and her own.

She sighed, feeling closer to him than ever before. Their two hearts were beating together, and somehow that made her feel a profound connection to him that was even stronger than the bond that had been created by sharing such rapturous lovemaking.

CHAPTER SEVEN

CLAUDIA awoke to the sound of the front door slamming, and then she heard footsteps crunching over the gravel outside the cottage. She was lying on the sofa, cocooned in the soft warmth of the duvet.

'The fog's cleared. We can get going at once,' Marco said, coming back inside with a blast of icy air.

Claudia struggled to sit up, still half asleep, and pulled the duvet tighter round her naked body.

She blinked and gazed blurrily at Marco. He was already dressed and looked as if he'd been up for hours. He'd always been like that, she remembered suddenly. He went from deep sleep to being fully awake in a split second. In the time they'd been together, he'd never once used an alarm clock.

She was the complete opposite—slow to wake up properly, even with an alarm buzzing. And she hated getting up in the cold. Marco, apparently, did not mind the cold.

'I won't take long to get ready,' she said, trying to gather the energy to move.

Marco looked down at Claudia as she turned sideways on the sofa to look up at him, dipping her head so that her hair fell forward past her shoulders to partially cover her breasts.

She looked the perfect image of a demure young lady who felt awkward and slightly bewildered at finding herself sitting naked next to a man the morning after a wild sexual encounter, now that the heat of the moment had passed.

Something about her innocent expression slid through Marco's nerves like a steel blade. He would never forget what she had done, or that she was preparing to marry Vasile.

Her face was still flushed from sleep as she stood up and stumbled round the room wrapped in the duvet, collecting her clothes. Then she headed to the bathroom.

Marco watched her go with an uncomfortable feeling of arousal burning through him.

The thought that he still wanted her disturbed him. He'd followed her to Wales and bedded her for revenge—to seek retribution for the way she had duped him. His intention had been to set the balance of power right—not to find himself driven to seek the delights of her body again, and again.

He knew what kind of woman she was.

He knew she had brought danger and corruption into his innocent sister's life. And right now—at this very moment—she was planning to marry the bastard who had destroyed his family, simply to get her hands on a large amount of money.

How could he want her in his bed, knowing that?

Because it was just sex. Incredible, mind-blowing sex.

Suddenly a nasty bolt of possessiveness surged through him. Primo Vasile would never have her! Not her money. And definitely not her body.

The money was not important to Marco—except that by keeping it from Vasile he would continue to hound his enemy further into desperate dire straits. But Claudia's body was a different matter. That would be his. Entirely his. Until he was utterly finished with it.

A few minutes later they were driving away from the cottage along the winding Pembrokeshire roads. A wind had picked up, blowing the fog away, and it was a bright, clear morning. A thick hoar-frost encrusted everything, covering the landscape with a silvery white hue, and when she turned round for one farewell glance Claudia saw that the sea was a dazzling cobalt blue.

Everything felt different from the day before. She was leaving the cottage in Marco's sports car, and would soon reach the airport where his private aeroplane was waiting for them. It was quite a change from the InterCity train and local bus she had travelled to Pembrokeshire in.

Later that day she would see her father. A whisper of dread coiled through her at the thought of how much he might have deteriorated since her last visit. But Marco would be there to talk to the doctors. Knowing he would be there, translating for her, gave her more strength.

Then the next day she would fly to the Caribbean to keep her end of her bargain with Vasile.

Part of her wanted to tell Marco. She felt guilty keeping it from him. But then, although they had spent the night together, she had no reason to trust him with such a huge personal secret. In fact, after what he'd said last night, she had every reason to believe that tomorrow he would be out of her life again, as completely as he had been four years ago.

A nasty, cold feeling of emptiness hung threateningly at the back of her mind, pressing forward whenever her thoughts strayed to the inevitable moment when he would leave her. But she tried to ignore it. Although she had taken comfort from being with Marco, and experienced bliss in his arms, she must not mistake their time together as more than it was. She had made that error four years ago and ended up with a broken heart.

Apart from just one night, Marco didn't want her. For her own protection, she must always remember that.

At least with Vasile she knew where she stood. He couldn't hurt her because she would never make herself vulnerable by opening her heart to him. He just wanted her money. He would never let her down, because she would never hope for more from him. There was nothing to lose except the money, which was meaningless to her.

She'd already lost everything that ever meant anything. And now she was losing her father. She had to do anything and everything possible to keep him safe and content during his final weeks and months.

Claudia sipped the velvety thick hot chocolate and closed her eyes in a moment of sheer, unadulterated pleasure. The deliciously rich hot chocolate was a matter of local pride in Turin. And it never failed to deliver—always providing comfort and a few minutes of escape from whatever life had thrown at her. She didn't know the recipe but it tasted just like pure melted chocolate, with maybe a dash of cream thrown in for good measure.

She'd first discovered it not long after coming to live in Italy. Her grandmother had just died, taking with her the only link she had with her real mother, and her father had recently become the business partner of a man called Primo Vasile— someone her stepmother, Francesca, had introduced him to. Claudia always had the impression that her father did not care for Vasile, but he seemed unable to refuse Francesca anything.

At first Claudia hadn't really liked Turin. Uprooted from her life in London, mourning the loss of her beloved grandmother and missing all her friends, Turin had seemed alien and unwelcoming. Francesca had brought her into the city on frequent shopping expeditions, under the pretence of helping her to adjust to her new life. But in reality she still had no time for her stepdaughter and usually left her alone, drinking hot chocolate, while she spent hours moving from one designer boutique on *Via Roma* to another.

After a while Claudia had become more confident and began to explore the city on her own. The first thing she realised was how friendly the people were. The next thing was that you could literally walk for miles under the elegant porticoes that lined so many of the grand streets around the city centre. In the height of the Italian summer they were always shady and cool, and on rainy or overcast days, when the clouds pressed in and you'd never know that the city was built so close to the looming mountains, you could still get about without needing an umbrella.

Now she was sitting in her favourite café in the *Quadrilatero Romano*, drinking hot chocolate while she waited for Marco to finish his business meeting. Then he would accompany her to the hospital and talk to her father's doctors.

It was a crisp clear day and the café was situated in an enchanting piazza in the shadow of an ancient bell tower. It was bustling with people and suddenly she was glad to be back in Turin. She liked it inside the traditional café. The jars of old-fashioned sweets lined up so colourfully behind the counter reminded her of her childhood, and the caring motherly ladies who ran the café made her feel safe.

Today she sat facing the door, looking out at the sunny

piazza. She wanted to be able to see Marco approaching. At last she spotted him walking across the piazza towards the café. Her heart gave a little leap of pleasure and suddenly, despite the crowds of people, it was as if there was no one else in the piazza.

He looked so impressive, dressed impeccably in a dark suit with a crisp white shirt. A gold watch and cufflinks glinted at his wrists and his Italian leather shoes gleamed. As he walked, people seemed to flow naturally out of his way. She sat up a little straighter, a feeling of pride swelling through her. That gorgeous man was walking towards her.

'*Ciao.*' He greeted her with a kiss and almost immediately a waitress was beside them, ready to take their order.

'How was your meeting?' Claudia asked once the waitress had gone, suppressing a smile at the admiring glances Marco was drawing from all the women in the café. She'd almost forgotten what it was like to be out in public with him, how every female eye turned his way, how every man he encountered seemed to jump to do his bidding.

'Excellent,' Marco said. 'In fact, I'm very pleased—I have everything I need to complete something I've been working towards for a long time.'

'You don't look all that pleased.' Claudia spoke without thinking as she took in the grim set of his face.

'It's not over yet.' He turned his gaze on to her and she was startled by the intensity in his dark eyes. 'I'll celebrate when it's done.'

She stared back at him and the coldness in his expression made an icy feeling wash over her. The thought crossed her mind that he seemed like a stranger, but then she'd always known he hadn't risen so high in the global business arena by being warm and fuzzy. She knew that he had a ruthless streak, a steely determination to get what he wanted.

'Will you be happy when it's done?' she asked. 'Or will you just start work on another deal?' It had never occurred to her before to wonder if Marco was happy. He'd always seemed so dynamic and in control that his happiness was something that she'd never questioned.

'This is not just any deal,' he said. Something in his voice told her that it really was something of great importance to him. It seemed strange to her that, given how intimate they had been, that she didn't know what it was that was so important to him.

'So you'll be extra happy when it's over?' she pushed.

'*Happiness* has nothing to do with it,' Marco grated. A muscle suddenly pulsed on his jaw line and a dangerous glint lit his eye. Claudia bit her lip, realising that she had intruded too far into matters that didn't concern her.

'Sorry,' she said. 'I didn't mean to pry.'

Just at that moment the waitress arrived, carrying a tray with their drinks.

Claudia fell silent and watched her place two short-stemmed glasses of the famous *bicerin* on the table, followed by two glasses of water.

'Now I know I'm in Turin.' Claudia slid her drink towards her, trying to lighten the atmosphere between them. After all, Marco was about to do her a great favour when he spoke to her father's doctors.

'We'll go straight to the hospital when we're finished here.' The tone of Marco's voice was back to normal and his expression was bland. But it was clear that he did not want to let their conversation return to the previous subject.

Claudia picked up her drink and took a sip, thinking about their approaching visit to the hospital. The *bicerin* was a Turinese speciality, a sublime creation of rich hot chocolate, espresso and whipped cream, carefully poured in layers into a glass. It was very rich and strong, and she had never tasted anything like it anywhere else.

Suddenly the coffee and chocolate mixture was too rich and strong for her.

'I'm sorry,' Claudia said, pushing the scarcely touched drink away from her and taking a sip of the water instead. 'I already had hot chocolate—I shouldn't have ordered anything else.'

Marco shrugged. Despite being a speciality of his home town, the *bicerin* wasn't to his taste—a double espresso was more his style. He'd been distracted when he'd ordered, thinking about the excellent report his legal team had given him.

Everything was in place now for him to take Vasile down. One phone call to the police was all it would take for Vasile and Francesca to be taken away for good.

But he wanted more than that. He wanted to be there when Vasile's world fell apart—to let him know that it was he, Marco De Luca, who had totally annihilated him, destroying everything he cared about in the process.

'Shall we go?' Marco tossed more than enough euros on to the table to cover their bill.

Claudia nodded and rose to her feet, looking pale and nervous. He realised she really was anxious about visiting her father. A strangely protective feeling ran through him, but he pushed it aside. He would not let her vulnerability blind him to what she was really like. He knew what she'd done in the past. And he knew what she was planning to do any day now—marry a man old enough to be her father, just to get her hands on her trust fund a few years early.

Marco stood up and followed her out of the café.

'He looked a lot better today,' Claudia said as she and Marco walked away from the hospital.

In fact she'd been surprised by just how well her father had seemed, compared to her last visit when he'd scarcely recognised her. It was a long time since he'd been able to sit up and talk to her properly. But he'd grown tired quickly, making her worried that he might overdo it. So, although she'd been reluctant to leave, once Marco had spoken to his doctors, they'd left him to rest.

'He *is* better,' Marco said. 'The last few times you saw him, he was suffering from a secondary infection that was resisting the doctors' best efforts to treat it. But now they've finally found the right balance of medication. Your father is responding well and the infection is on its way to being cleared up.'

'I don't understand.' She paused and turned to look at Marco. 'Francesca never mentioned anything about that.'

'Claudia, somehow you have been given the wrong impression,' Marco said. He stopped walking and turned to face her. 'Your father's condition is *not* terminal. It is serious and his recovery will take a while—but there is no reason to expect him not to get better.'

'But…how?' She stumbled for words, finding it hard to comprehend what Marco was telling her.

'I don't know how the misunderstanding came about,' he said. 'But your father is not dying.'

Claudia stared at Marco in utter shock. Her father was not dying. Her father was *not* dying!

A bubble of joy started rising up through her body but she pressed her teeth into her lower lip, almost afraid to smile. She drew in a long shaky breath. Was it really true?

'Are you sure?' she asked Marco tremulously. 'Are *they* sure—the doctors, I mean?'

'It's true,' Marco said. 'The doctors are completely sure. There has never been any question that his condition was terminal.'

A massive smile broke across Claudia's face and she felt a burst of happiness swelling inside her. It was as if a colossal weight that had been relentlessly dragging her down from inside her soul had been lifted off her—her father was not dying. Everything was going to be all right.

'I can't believe it!' she gasped, throwing her arms instinctively around Marco. 'Oh, thank you. Thank you so much for telling me!'

'You're welcome,' Marco said, automatically returning her embrace. 'I'm pleased that he is not so ill as you thought.'

His words sounded stiff and formal to his own ears, but they were soon engulfed in her happiness. The positive emotion that she was radiating was almost tangible—like a real physical thing that was emanating from her and wrapping around them both as she clung to him in her relief. She was glowing so warm and bright that for a moment he actually felt her happiness penetrating his heart too.

It was a disconcerting feeling. But then he suddenly felt a shudder run through her body.

He held her away from him, instinctively looking into her face, and saw that her eyes were sparkling with tears of happiness and relief.

'You don't have to worry about him any more,' he said, brushing his thumb gently across her cheek.

'I can hardly believe it,' she whispered. 'It feels so good.'

Marco smiled at her. It was a totally natural response to her joyous emotion—he felt happy on her behalf.

But why had Claudia believed her father was dying when it wasn't true? Her tears in Wales had certainly seemed genuine.

When he'd told her what the doctors had said, he'd watched the expression on her face change slowly from confusion, through disbelief and finally to pure joy. It was clear from her reaction that she really had believed her father to be terminally ill.

It was inconceivable that she had been so wrong about something so important. The possibility that Francesca Hazelton had deliberately misled Claudia flashed through his mind. It would be an appalling thing to do—but then Francesca and Vasile had done far worse things over the years.

'Will you take me out to my father's home in the countryside?' Claudia asked suddenly. 'He asked me to fetch him some of his things and I said I'd bring them to him.'

Marco stared at her, a sudden jolt of shock running through him.

Was she insane?

Had the joy of discovering her father wasn't terminally ill made her lose her mind? She must have momentarily forgotten *who* she was talking to—why else would she have asked him to take her out to the family estate?

The very same estate that had belonged to Marco's family before Claudia's family had taken it away from them.

'I'm sorry,' Claudia said, looking intently at his face. 'I didn't mean to impose—you've done enough already.'

Marco looked at her, deliberately eliminating all signs of emotion from his face. He had obviously been too quick to think that someone else was manipulating her. He *would* take her out to the estate that should rightfully belong to him—that would soon belong to him again.

Twelve years ago he had vowed that he would never set foot there again—not until his revenge was complete. But that glorious day was as good as here.

'I apologise,' Marco said. 'I was distracted for a minute. Of course I'll take you. If we leave now, we can be back in the city this evening.'

'There's no need—not if you're too busy with that important business you mentioned at the café,' Claudia said. 'I can find my own way there.'

'I said I'll take you there.' The decision had been made.

CHAPTER EIGHT

THEY left the city in the middle of the afternoon to drive out to Hector Hazelton's home in the Piedmont countryside. Marco's face was set in a grim expression.

He didn't know how he felt about returning to the estate where he'd grown up. He'd been working towards reclaiming the property for twelve years, but this visit was unexpected. It was not how he'd imagined his return would take place.

A lot had happened during the intervening time. When he was eighteen years old he had already been making a start in the world of business—wanting to break away from the father he didn't get along with and prove himself to his beloved grandfather. Now he was a billionaire—a significant player on a global scale that even his grandfather and father wouldn't recognise.

As he drove Claudia along the Piedmont roads that he remembered so well, he felt strangely detached. The roads looked familiar, but it was as if he didn't really know them. He couldn't recall what it was like—*how he'd felt*—driving along those roads during his youth, before Vasile had destroyed his family.

All he could remember was how he'd felt the terrible day he'd driven home—except it was no longer home—to take responsibility for his eleven-year-old sister. The gut-wrenching anger that had consumed him that day had never gone.

Now, years later, Marco had everything he needed to bring down Primo Vasile and Francesca Hazelton, and to reclaim the property where he'd grown up. Francesca was the legal owner of the estate, although it was her husband, Hector, who had made his home there.

Marco had never found anything he could use against Hector. As far as he could tell, Claudia's father was an honest businessman and, although he had moved his own family on to the estate after the De Lucas were gone, he had not been directly involved in the ruin of Marco's family.

He'd taken over the management of the vineyard and Marco knew that Hector had been a good employer—the loyal staff who'd worked for the De Luca family had not suffered unnecessarily. Marco frowned, thinking that, like his own father, Hector Hazelton would have been better off without his wife. Francesca was a lying, deceiving witch, just like Marco's mother. Just like Claudia.

Marco wished Hector no harm, but he had no qualms about taking back his home. Hector had his own assets in England and would still be a wealthy man. It was too bad he hadn't chosen a better second wife. Then perhaps his daughter wouldn't have turned out to be a corrupt schemer like her stepmother.

'It's just round the next bend, on the right,' Claudia said, as if she was unaware that Marco did not need directions.

He swung his sports car into the tree-lined avenue that led to the house and his heart started to thump heavily, like the slow, steady beat of a military drum within his cold chest. His grandfather had planted those trees as a wedding gift for his wife. Marco could barely remember his grandmother; she had died when he was a young boy. But he remembered his grandfather very well. The old man would probably still be alive if it hadn't been for Vasile.

'We've made good time,' Claudia added, looking at her watch. 'We should be halfway back to the city before it gets dark.'

Marco barely registered her words. He was thinking about his beloved grandfather— another innocent victim of Vasile's corruption. He had died the night Marco's father, drunk on a lethal combination of shame and alcohol, had driven his car off the road.

Marco had not been there to stop it.

That was his biggest regret.

'I'm so glad my father was well enough to ask for some of his things.' Claudia's voice right beside him jolted him out of his thoughts.

'Yes.' The single word was all he could manage, with the memory of his grandfather's needless death fresh in his mind.

Claudia jumped eagerly out of the car and hurried up to the front door as if she couldn't wait to get inside. He stood still, looking up at the traditional Piedmont property that until twelve years ago had been in his family for generations. It was a fine day and the majestic mountains in the north were clearly visible. They provided a never-changing, solid point of reference but, as he looked, nothing about the house, or the garden that was visible from his viewpoint, appeared to have changed.

And, as he stood there staring, a battery of other memories hammered through to the front of his mind. He felt every muscle in his body tighten.

The door opened almost before Claudia had reached it and Marco realised that someone inside must have seen the car approaching. An older lady appeared, presumably the housekeeper, and laughter and greetings followed. Then suddenly the friendly chatter ceased. Everything had gone silent.

'Signor De Luca?' The woman who had welcomed Claudia was staring at him as if she had seen a ghost.

'I'm sorry,' Claudia said, looking almost as startled as the older lady. 'Let me introduce you. Rosa, this is Marco De Luca. He was kind enough to drive me out here from the city today.'

Marco studied the kindly-looking woman who was staring at him with her eyes as wide as saucers, and suddenly he realised who she was. Or rather where they had encountered each other before. She was one of the many people who had been employed by his parents to run the house, back when the estate had belonged to them.

'Rosa—' Marco stepped forward and surprised her by taking her hand '—how good to see you looking so well. How are you? And your sons? They must be grown up by now.'

'Very well,' Rosa stammered. 'Everyone is well. Paolo, my oldest, is engaged to be married next year.'

'Congratulations,' Marco said. 'I am sure you are very proud.'

He glanced at Claudia and saw that she was following the exchange with a bewildered expression.

'Rosa used to work for my parents,' Marco explained, watching her carefully to see her reaction.

'But…Rosa, I thought you'd worked in this house since you were a young girl?' Claudia said. Her cheeks were flushed and there was a mixture of confusion and disbelief on her face.

'*Si*, that's right,' Rosa said. 'Before you came here, the estate was owned by the De Luca family.'

For a moment Claudia forgot to breathe.

She stared at Marco, hoping to see some indication that this…this *coincidence* had been as much of a surprise to him as it had been to her. But there was nothing. No surprise. No awkwardness.

He had always known about this link between them.

'Oh, my God!' she cried. 'You knew all along!' She clapped her hand over her mouth and fled into the house. She ran instinctively to her father's study and opened the window, gasping for air.

'Don't be so dramatic.' She heard Marco's scornful voice behind her and spun round in time to see him closing the door of the study. 'You knew as well as I did about our little connection.'

'*Little connection*!' Claudia exclaimed. 'We grew up in the same house! And, although *you* clearly knew that, you never saw fit to mention it to me.'

'Why tell you something you already knew?' Marco asked. 'You obviously wanted to pretend that you were unaware of us—of Bianca, of me—of all of the people who were torn apart by the unscrupulous dealings of your family. At the time it suited my purpose to go along with that.'

'I don't know what you are talking about.' Claudia stared at him with wide eyes, struggling to comprehend what was happening. 'What unscrupulous dealings? What do you mean by *torn apart*?'

She couldn't understand the accusations he seemed to be making. And, as she stared at his hostile expression, it felt as if she hardly recognised him. Had he truly believed such appalling things about her all the time they'd known each other?

'You can give up the lies now,' Marco grated. 'You have nothing to gain by continuing to keep up the pretence.'

'I haven't been lying to you,' Claudia said.

She was shocked to discover that her family had moved

into the house that had once been the home of the De Lucas. It was hard to believe, but it must be true—after all, Rosa had confirmed it.

In that case, Claudia could understand why there might be hard feelings. But Marco seemed to be accusing her of something much worse. He really seemed to think that Bianca, and the rest of his family, had been deliberately hurt by her family.

'There is no point in clinging to your petty fiction,' Marco said. The disdain that dripped from his voice matched the expression on his hard face. 'It's time to move on from that now—get it all out in the open at last.'

'Everything I've ever told you is true.' Claudia felt her eyes fill with tears but she blinked them away and faced him squarely. 'I trusted you with so many things—things that really mattered to me. And you repaid that trust with deception.'

'I didn't lie to you,' Marco said angrily. 'I simply didn't tell you the whole of my life story.'

'What's the difference?' she asked. 'It comes to the same thing if you deliberately mislead someone.'

'I was simply playing you at your own game,' Marco responded.

'I wasn't playing a game. My friendship with Bianca was genuine, and I believed that what you and I had together was genuine,' she said. Then, suddenly, an awful thought occurred to her. 'Did Bianca know too? Is that why she dropped me?'

'I stopped her contacting you,' Marco said. 'I took her away to America, to get her as far from you as possible.'

'I felt so bad when you disappeared,' Claudia said. 'I thought you didn't care any more—that you had better things to do. Now I know that you wanted to hurt me! That you were laughing at me!'

'I was never laughing at you. It was never that trivial.' He looked at her coldly, through dangerously narrowed eyes.

'If Rosa hadn't recognised you, I still wouldn't know about your family.' Claudia stood tall and looked straight back at him, although a horrible threatening sensation scratched down her spine as their eyes met.

'I was going to bring everything into the open today,' Marco said.

'Why today?' she said. 'Why should I believe you were finally going to reveal your awful secret today?'

'My awful secret?' Marco bit out, echoing her words. He clenched his fists by his sides, suddenly seeing red. How dared she stand there and continue to pretend ignorance? 'You know the bare facts of the story as well as I do. What you don't know is what it was really like for my family when it happened.'

Her face was as white as a sheet as she looked up at him. He could tell she was shaken by their confrontation, but he didn't care. He wanted her to feel the pain he had felt—the pain he still felt when he remembered what had happened.

'Of course I don't know what it was like—I don't even know what happened,' she said in her defence.

'You don't know how many nights I lay awake—tortured by thoughts that perhaps I could have saved my family from the worst of it,' he said bitterly. 'Or maybe even could have prevented it altogether.'

'Prevented what?' she asked, still acting as if she didn't know what had taken place.

'The destruction of my family,' he said.

There was an ominous pause and his words seemed to echo around the room. Marco watched as a change came over her. Her body stiffened and suddenly she was standing very still.

'*Destruction*,' she said at last. 'That's a very strong word. How were your family destroyed?'

Her voice was so quiet and shaky that he could hardly hear her. But that didn't matter. He was on a roll now. He was going to tell her something that had been weighing on him for twelve years.

He wanted her to share his pain at the memory. He wanted her to feel his guilt over not stopping what happened.

'The last time I saw my father alive he was sitting at that very desk. He was drunk,' he said, raking his fingers roughly through his hair. 'He was bawling into his drink, saying that my mother was having an affair.'

He paused for a moment as an image of that scene flared horribly in his mind.

'He told me the family business and estate were in danger,' Marco continued. 'I didn't take him seriously. I was ashamed of him—disgusted that he was drinking and that he couldn't hold on to his wife. I told him to pull himself together.'

'You must have been very young.' Claudia's voice revealed her shock. 'What did he expect you to do? What *could* you have done to make a difference?'

'I was a man—eighteen years old. Old enough to take responsibility. I may not have known that my family was on the brink of destruction—or that a man called Primo Vasile had seduced my mother and persuaded her to betray my father. But I did know that my father was upset.' Marco paused, his heart pumping fiercely under his ribs. 'I didn't know what I could do to help. So I stuck to what I already had planned and left the country.'

Claudia didn't say anything. She just stared up at him with a stunned expression on her face.

'When I returned, everything had gone to hell,' Marco said. 'My father and grandfather were dead. My mother had fled in shame. And Bianca, my sweet, innocent little sister, was a virtual orphan, living at the mercy of state care.'

He turned away, looking blindly out of the window. The pain and shame that he normally kept so well clamped down seared into him like a brand. He had failed his family. And they—not him—had paid dearly for that failure.

'How did they die?' Claudia gasped.

'A car accident,' Marco bit out. 'My father should never have been driving. If I'd been here, I would have prevented it.'

'It's not your fault,' Claudia said. Despite the way he had just treated her, there was a sympathetic note in her voice. Sympathy was the last thing Marco wanted to hear.

'No—it's Vasile's fault,' Marco said.

'How awful,' Claudia said. 'For everyone—especially Bianca. She never told me anything about that.'

'Don't talk about my sister as if you care.' Marco rounded on her. 'That's where all this started between us.'

Claudia stared at him, utterly stunned by what Marco had told her.

Patches of livid red burned on his cheeks and he glared back at her with eyes that were full of accusation. His shoulders were trembling and she realised that he was consumed by a terrible combination of guilt and fury.

It was almost too much to take in. He had told her the night before that his mother had betrayed his family and abandoned Bianca, but she had never imagined that he was talking about such a cataclysmic outcome for the entire family.

The fact that Primo Vasile had been his mother's seducer, the catalyst behind all the destruction, was an appalling discovery. She knew he was a bad person—after all, he was blackmailing her into marriage—but the dark picture Marco had painted made her feel dizzy with horror that he had embroiled her in his schemes.

'I don't understand why you kept all this secret from me,' she said.

It had wrenched her heart when he'd told her how his family had suffered, but it wasn't fair of him to blame her. She'd been thirteen years old when it had happened. And she was still reeling from the shock of discovering that their families were connected in such an awful way.

'We both kept secrets,' Marco countered.

'I never deliberately withheld information,' Claudia said. 'In fact I *did* tell you everything—you always knew the names of my parents and where I came from. I didn't hide anything.'

'You never mentioned Primo Vasile,' Marco said. 'Don't you think that's a fairly major omission?'

'What did he have to do with me?' Claudia asked. Her blood ran cold—but it was only in the last couple of days that she'd had any direct involvement with him. 'Did you expect me to discuss every one of my father's business associates?'

Suddenly she stopped and stared at him in shock.

'That's what it was always about!' she gasped. 'You got close to me, hoping to find out information to use against Primo—because of what he did to your family.'

'No,' Marco said. 'Not then. I wanted to know what *you* were doing hanging round my sister.'

'She was my friend!' Claudia declared.

She glared at him, horrified that he could even imagine she might have had any other reason than friendship for spending time with his sister. Just what sort of person did he take her for? And what sort of person was *he* to judge her by such awful standards?

'Is Primo Vasile your friend?' he asked blandly.

'I hardly know him,' she snapped, still smarting from his insinuation that she had somehow been a threat to his sister.

'Maybe not the best basis for marriage,' he said.

CHAPTER NINE

CLAUDIA'S heart lurched.

Somehow Marco knew about her planned marriage to Primo.

'No...I...' she stammered. She wanted to deny it—it had been such a hard struggle to accept that she must go through with it. Having Marco throw it in her face was unbearable.

'Do you think I'm a complete fool?' Marco demanded. 'I've made it my business to know everything that bastard does. I know everything he so much as thinks, even before he knows it himself. Something like a wedding would never escape my notice.'

'But how...?' Claudia's voice died away. It was only two days since she'd met Primo and Francesca at the Ritz, and that was the first time the subject of her marriage to Primo had been raised. Or, rather, that was when they had used her father's precarious situation to blackmail her into marriage.

Marco had appeared right outside the Ritz only moments later. Somehow he had known about it before she had.

She clamped both hands over her face, feeling sick to her stomach. She had been used. By everyone.

Francesca and Vasile had used her—were still planning to use her. She'd tried to shut that appalling reality away, not think about it because there was nothing she could do about it. She had to go through with it, for the sake of her father. But now the discovery that Marco had been using her too was overwhelming.

'There's no need to hide, *bella mia*.' She felt Marco's fingers on her wrists, pulling her hands away from her face. 'The fact that you are not what you seem to be is nothing new to me. I know what the face of deception looks like.'

A sudden wave of anger washed over her, heating her blood, making her back straighter. She whipped her hands down, jerking her wrists free of Marco's grip and lifted her chin in defiance.

'You are despicable,' she said.

'As despicable as falling into another man's bed only days before your wedding?' he sneered.

'You knew—but still you…' She drew in a shuddering breath. 'I felt so guilty. I tried to stop it, but you were so…persistent.'

'You wanted it as much as I did,' he reminded her.

'You set me up!' Claudia cried. 'Appearing outside the Ritz. Following me to Wales.'

'You ought to be used to set-ups,' Marco said. 'But you don't like it when the tables are turned on you. Personally, I rather enjoyed myself. And I thought there was a certain poetic justice in the location—Wales always was special for us.'

Claudia's head was throbbing and her mind spinning with what she was hearing. She'd never seen Marco behave like this before. Had never heard him use such a harsh tone of voice. Had never heard him say such cruel things.

'You're so different,' she said, running her eyes over him almost desperately, as if by looking hard enough she might see some sign of the Marco who had meant so much to her. 'I don't even recognise the man in front of me.'

'Is this better?' he asked, stripping off his jacket, then his shirt.

'What are you doing?' She stared in shock at his naked torso. Her heart started to beat out a rhythm of alarm and a surge of adrenaline flooded her body.

'This is how you've seen me most frequently over the last couple of days,' Marco said. 'I thought seeing me like this might help you get things in perspective.'

'I've got everything in perfect perspective,' she snapped, thinking just how much her world had changed in a matter of minutes. 'Thank you for showing me, in case I hadn't fully realised yet, just how much of a brute you are.'

She straightened her shoulders, refusing to take even one step backwards, although part of her wanted to turn tail and flee. Another darker, instinct driven part of her wanted to let her eyes roam over his naked skin. But she kept her head up, meeting his gaze steadily with her own.

She was wearing the smart high-heeled shoes she'd changed into for a day in the city, giving her three inches of extra height, but still he towered over her, making her feel shorter than she was.

'You do realise nothing has changed,' Marco said. 'We are still the same people we were half an hour ago. You're the same woman who made love to me, only days before her wedding.'

'It wasn't like that,' Claudia protested. 'I would never have done that if...' She bit her lip—it was so hard to explain. 'The wedding—it's not what you think.'

'What do I think it is?' Marco asked smoothly.

'It's just a business arrangement,' she said.

'Is that better than the alternative?' Marco asked. 'The traditional reason for marriage—that you've fallen in love.'

Claudia dropped her gaze, suddenly flustered.

There was another alternative—blackmail. But she couldn't tell him that. If she did, he would discover the power Vasile had over her. Then he could take that power and use it for himself.

The man she'd thought he was would never do such a thing, but now she knew he was ruthless and had no honour. She could never expose her father to him.

'It's not going to be that kind of wedding—it will be platonic, a business arrangement only.' Claudia lifted her hand and pushed her hair off her face.

'To get your hands on your trust fund five years early,' Marco said derisively.

'How do you know about my trust fund?' Claudia said in shock. Her father had always kept it quiet to protect her from people interested in her only for the money she would have one day.

'I told you—I've made it my business to know these things,' Marco said. 'I suppose you've had enough of working for a living and can't wait for the money.'

'It's not that simple,' she said. 'I need the money for something really important.'

'And what does Vasile get out of it?' he asked in a way that made a nasty prickle of distaste run down between her shoulder blades.

'Nothing,' she said automatically, then realised that wouldn't sound very convincing. 'Well, some money, of course.'

'Only money?' Marco said incredulously, letting his eyes roam across her suggestively. 'You're not naive enough to think Vasile won't want to taste the delights of that body himself?'

'You're disgusting!' she gasped, suddenly feeling the blood drain away from her head, making her feel dizzy with shock. The very idea of it made her feel sick. That was not what she had agreed to. She would *never* agree to something like that.

'You've done a deal with the devil—what did you expect?' Marco said harshly. 'You can't seriously think he won't take everything he can get?'

'Not that!' she gasped, feeling her stomach turn over in revulsion.

'Don't worry about it,' Marco said, lifting a hand and slipping it into her hair. 'Vasile's never going to get a chance to lay a finger on you.'

'What…what do you mean?' Claudia stammered.

A shudder of apprehension suddenly rippled through her and at the same time she became ultra aware of his hand in her hair. She tried to take a step backwards, but Marco responded instantly, slipping his hand to the back of her head to hold her in place.

'I'm not letting him have you,' he said.

He was so close that she could feel the heat radiating off his naked chest. See the subtle flare of his ribcage as he breathed.

'It's got nothing to do with you.' She fidgeted under his intense gaze, unsettled by how breathless her own voice sounded. His eyes were boring down into her, penetrating the defensive barrier of emotional control she was trying to hold up against him.

'It has everything to do with me,' he said, pulling her slightly nearer to him. 'You're mine now.'

Claudia's eyes widened and she swallowed nervously. Her body was already responding to the sexual message in Marco's words—and that was the last thing she wanted.

'You've just spent the last few minutes telling me what a terrible person I am,' she said. 'Why would you care if I married a man you hate?'

'Vasile is not having you,' he grated. 'He'll never have you.'

'You don't want me,' she whispered.

'You know I do. And you still want me,' he goaded her.

'No!' She denied it. 'How could I want someone so heart-less—someone who was using me all along?'

'I don't know, *bella mia*,' Marco said, skimming his hand down the back of her neck and slipping it under the soft collar of her blouse. Then he slowly drew it flat against the skin across her shoulder, around to the base of her throat. 'Maybe because you're not the kind of girl who marries for love.'

Tears sparkled in Claudia's eyes as she looked at him. How could she challenge him? She had just told him she was marrying for business reasons. And, despite all the deception between them, she knew there was some truth in his words now. She did still want him.

His hand was burning against her skin, slipping lower and lower against her breastbone with every shallow breath she took. She had to stop him—but she didn't want to.

'Don't do this.' Her voice was shaky and she knew it lacked conviction.

'We've been here before,' Marco reminded her harshly, 'when you begged me in the shower not to take your clothes off. Then, later, you were writhing in my arms as I made love to you.'

'That won't happen now,' Claudia said, trying to pull his hand away from the inside of her blouse. But his reactions were too quick and she found her own hand pinned beneath his, flat against the skin above her left breast. She could feel her heart beating beneath her palm and the iron strength of his grasp as he held her hand in place.

'I know it will,' Marco said, lifting his free hand and starting to undo the front of her blouse. 'But I don't have time to play any more games. We have a flight to catch to the Caribbean and must be on our way back to the city soon.'

'I'm not going to the Caribbean with you!' Claudia gasped, barely aware of his fingers making quick work of her buttons. Did he know absolutely everything—even that she was supposed to meet Francesca and Vasile in the Caribbean? 'I…I've made a commitment. I have to see it through.'

'You're coming with me,' he said.

'But why?' she said, desperately trying to think of a way she could protect her father. If she didn't marry Primo Vasile as she had agreed, Vasile would turn her father in to the police.

'I plan to take everything from Vasile.' Marco's eyes were gleaming dangerously, setting Claudia's sense of self-protection on to red alert. 'Every little thing that is of any importance to him. And you are one of those things.'

'I'm not a thing!' Claudia's voice quavered, but she squared her shoulders and stood up taller. The slight movement made her aware of her own hand just above her breast, with Marco's hand pressing over it. But she carried on, determined to defend herself. 'And I'm not important to Vasile.'

'Your trust fund is,' Marco said brutally.

'It's only money,' she replied.

'Money he desperately needs,' Marco said. 'Money he thinks will save him.'

'From you?' Claudia's voice was small.

'He doesn't know it's me,' Marco said. 'I've been squeezing him dry, pressuring him from all sides, waiting for him to make a mistake.'

She stared up at him, appalled all over again by what she was hearing. He was consumed by his need for revenge and she was to be part of that. His conquest of her was linked in his mind to the destruction of the man who had ruined his family.

'It was Vasile who hurt your family, not me,' she said. 'What have I ever done to you to make you treat me like this?'

'Enough,' Marco said, suddenly closing the distance between them and bringing his mouth down on hers.

For a fraction of a second she wondered what he meant by the word *enough*. Did he mean that she'd done enough to deserve his revenge, or that they'd done enough talking?

Then all her thoughts were blown away as a surge of sensation rose up through her body. Marco was plundering her mouth with a kiss that was forceful and possessive. And incredibly erotic.

She tried to pull away but hot arousal sizzled along her nerve endings, obliterating any thought of resistance from her mind. She felt his hands sweeping quickly over her, striping off her blouse, unhooking her bra. Then reaching under her skirt to tug down her lacy briefs.

The next moment he lifted her on to the wide leather topped desk, pushing things out of the way impatiently. She was lying on her back with her knees bent. Her skirt had ridden up to show the wide band of lace at the top of her hold-ups and she was still wearing her high-heeled shoes. She moved her feet, intending to kick them off.

'Leave them on,' Marco commanded, pushing forward between her legs so that he was kneeling over her, his arms braced on either side of her shoulders.

She stared up at him, hearing her own breath already coming in shallow gasps as she anticipated his lovemaking.

All the unpleasant emotions that had been raging through her only minutes earlier seemed to have been converted into hot, physical desire. Maybe it was a subconscious act of protection against more pain. Or maybe it was simply that she still burned with sexual longing for Marco. Whatever the reason, she was suddenly desperate for him to make love to her.

His black hair fell down over his forehead, but it did not soften his appearance. His dark eyes were narrowed with intent and there was a fierce set to his jaw line.

Without saying a word, he dipped forward and took her nipple deep into his mouth. He kissed it roughly, drawing it into a diamond-hard peak of throbbing sensation. Then he moved to the other breast and repeated his actions. Her whole body trembled and she arched her back, pressing her shoulders down against the hard surface of the desk and thrusting her breasts up towards him.

Then he pulled back and in one fluid movement dropped down so that his head was between her legs.

Claudia gasped and tried to sit up, suddenly unnerved by that extra level of intimacy. But his hands were moving, pushing her back down on the desk, then forcing her skirt higher, before sliding round to hold on to her bottom to keep her still.

A moment later his mouth found the most sensitive place on her body.

'Oh!' The moan of pure sexual pleasure tore from deep within her lungs and she flexed her feet, digging her heels down and instinctively tilting her pelvis up towards him.

His tongue glided over her quivering flesh, teasing her mercilessly, making her body writhe beneath him. She rocked her hips, almost unable to bear the intensity of the pleasure he was giving her, but he held her tight.

He kept his mouth pressed against her flesh, continuing to stimulate her with exquisite movements of his tongue and lips. It felt like the most intimate possession of her body she had ever known. As if somehow Marco was right inside her being, driving her experience from within.

He was in total control of her body. Every flick of his tongue sent waves of bliss undulating through her. There was nothing she could do but surrender to it—surrender to him.

She felt as if she were flying, soaring out of her body into the heavens. Marco kept on, driving her relentlessly towards her ultimate release. Then suddenly, magically, she reached the highest point.

A shimmering moment of rapture took her, bursting though her body like a million points of light, transporting her to another wonderful place.

For a moment she lost all awareness of her surroundings and she didn't feel Marco pulling away from her. The next thing she knew, he was lying over her, pressing in between her parted legs, positioning himself to thrust deep into her body.

She was still floating halfway between the heavens and earth and her muscles felt weak and shaky, but she reached up to grip his shoulders and lifted her legs to wrap them around his hips.

Then, with one perfect movement, he drove himself into her.

'Oh, Marco!'

A renewed burst of pleasure took hold of her and she cried out his name. She didn't know that it was possible to go any higher than she already had, but with every powerful thrust he was carrying her upwards, beyond anything she had ever even dreamed of.

A torrent of molten pleasure surged through her helpless body, making her tremble and moan. She clung to him, every inch of her vibrating with the red-hot energy that was pulsing within her.

Overwhelming sensations spiralled out from where their bodies were joined, and the feelings were building—growing stronger and stronger. Like a force of nature, Marco possessed her body, taking her to a place so wonderful that nothing but pleasure existed. He was thrusting faster and faster, harder and harder into her.

Suddenly Claudia cried out and dug her fingers into his back. Her inner muscles contracted, clenching tightly around him, drawing him deeper still. And her world exploded into a rainbow of glittering stars.

Then, a moment later, Marco gave a ferocious shout as he reached his climax.

It was only a couple of minutes later when Marco lifted himself away from Claudia. He got dressed without speaking and then turned his back on her to look out of the window.

The estate stretched out below him, towards the jagged peaks of the Alps. Earlier, when they'd arrived, everything had looked the same. But now the long winter shadows and the burnished light of the approaching sunset made it hard for him to recognise anything. In his memory he had always seen the property in the hazy brightness of high summer, with the grapes ripening on the vine and his sister riding her pony.

But whether the view he saw today matched his memory didn't matter—he'd worked for this for so long, and now it was nearly in his grasp.

He found himself looking down at the fountain courtyard—she same place he'd seen in Claudia's photographs in Wales. He'd been looking at that photo of Hector, thinking about taking back what rightfully belonged to him. Then he had turned and seen Claudia weeping.

An unexpected jolt of emotion spiked through him as he remembered how sad and vulnerable she had looked. He could still see her face—her wide golden brown eyes glistening with tears and her full sensual lips quivering as she'd tried not to cry, tried not to let him see how upset she was.

Then she had told him Hector was dying, and she had clung to him and wept, letting all her feelings out. He'd responded automatically to her distress, which had seemed so genuine, so deeply heartfelt. For a moment he'd felt himself softening towards her, until he'd remembered everything she had done. Weeping for her father did not cancel out the way she had preyed on his innocent sister. Or the way she'd played him—setting him up, getting him out of the country so that Vasile could get his hands on Bianca.

Anger suddenly surged through him. Claudia deserved whatever she got. And he hadn't finished with her yet.

He heard quiet noises as she started to get up coming from the desk behind him. He was surprised. Her orgasm had been so intense that he hadn't expected her to be moving so soon.

'Oh!'

The sound of her gasp made him spin round immediately.

She was sitting on the edge of the desk in a state of instantly arousing disarray. Naked to the waist, a gloriously untidy curtain of coppery hair hung past her shoulders, partially hiding her breasts in a way that made him itch to slip his hands beneath its silky weight and cup her soft flesh. Her skirt was rucked up over her hips, showing her long slender legs right past the lacy tops of her stockings. And, amazingly, she was still wearing those sexy high-heeled shoes.

He dragged his eyes away from her body and looked at her face. The second he made eye contact she spoke.

'I hate you!' she spat out.

'How refreshingly honest,' Marco drawled, despite the unexpectedly painful way her words stabbed into him. 'To be able to speak the plain truth will be a relief. It was growing tedious thinking up new ways to flatter you. At least now we both know where we stand.'

She stared up at him, her flashing eyes showing nothing but anger as she slid off the edge of the desk and stood facing him.

'Come here and look at what's happened!' she demanded, pointing to the top of the desk where several ugly gouges scarred the leather and wood. 'You knew that would happen. You made me leave my stilettos on deliberately.'

Marco looked down at the gouges dispassionately. It had never occurred to him that that would be a possible outcome of leaving her shoes on.

'Believe me, damaging the desk was the last thing on my mind,' he said, remembering the erotic sight of her lying there half naked, bare breasts heaving, ready for the taking.

'It was another part of your revenge,' she accused him. 'Deliberately defacing my father's property.'

'Your family took over the house fully furnished,' he grated. 'That was *my* father's desk before it was your father's. And, trust me, deflowering his daughter was far more satisfying than vandalising his furniture.'

A wave of heightened colour washed across her skin, but she stood her ground, continuing to glare up at him.

'How can you be so heartless?' she asked. 'With any luck

he'll be coming out of hospital soon. What's he going to think when he sees that?' She gestured towards the scarred desktop.

'Look on the bright side,' he said. 'At least he's not dying.'

There was a sickening pause, his words hanging in the air for a moment before Claudia responded.

'You beast!' she gasped.

The look in her eyes seared into him like a poisoned blade and a cold wave of self-disgust crashed through him.

He was about to apologise —a comment like that could never be justified, no matter what a person had done. But then she rounded on him again, before he had a chance to speak.

'Is there no blow too low?' she demanded furiously. 'Are there no depths you won't sink to in your crusade against my family?'

Her question struck deep, far too close to the bone for comfort, but his pride forced him to stare back at her steadily, not letting her see any reaction.

'You bring out the worst in me.' He shrugged, ignoring the slash of heat he felt burning on his cheeks.

'I still want to collect the things my father asked for,' Claudia said, picking up her bra and putting it on in front of him, without any sign of modesty about her body.

That was a change from before, Marco realised. She seemed more confident in her actions. Normally she dressed shyly, trying to keep her body covered as much as possible while she struggled awkwardly into her clothes. He'd always liked watching her, finding it endearing. After all, if she was getting dressed, that probably meant they'd just been completely naked, making love.

Now she seemed almost like a different person. It was as if bringing everything out into the open between them meant she no longer had to put on an act for him.

That thought bothered him a disproportionate amount. He'd always known she was a liar. But he did not like the idea that even little things, like the way she got dressed, had not been real.

'Make it quick,' he said, turning away to pick up his jacket.

He had to get out of the house. Just being there was messing with his head—making him lose his focus.

'Your back!' he heard Claudia gasp and he turned towards her. 'There's blood on your shirt,' she said.

He twisted round and looked in the large mirror that hung over the traditional fireplace. Sure enough, there were three streaks of blood on one of his shoulder blades, seeping through scarlet-red against his white shirt. Claudia must have dug her nails into his back when he'd brought her to the point of ecstasy.

'It looks like the desk wasn't the only thing to get gouged,' he said.

The sight of her mortified face in the mirror made him do a double take, but when he spun around to look at her properly she had erased her expression.

'I hope it stings,' she said coldly.

Then a moment later she ducked down to pick up her lacy briefs from the floor, but not before he'd seen her expression return to one of embarrassment and discomfort.

'Hurry,' he said. 'We have to get out of here.'

He was suddenly keen to be on his way back to the city. Claudia might have seen another side of herself when she'd realised she'd dug her fingernails into his back while they were making love.

But he was unsettled for an altogether different reason. Since they'd arrived at the house, he'd seen a side of himself he didn't much like.

CHAPTER TEN

CLAUDIA stared at the Piedmont countryside slipping past outside the car window through a haze of unshed tears. She bit her lip, refusing to cry. She would not give Marco that satisfaction.

But when she let herself think about everything that had happened that afternoon, and about all the awful things she had discovered, she felt as if she were falling into a monstrous black hole—as if she were being crushed into oblivion, until there was nothing left of her.

It was impossible to come to terms with everything. There was too much to take in and she simply couldn't process it all.

Earlier that day, when Marco had told her that her father wasn't dying, she'd been so happy. For a brief moment it had felt, somehow, that she'd got her own life back—as if things could return to normal.

Then she'd remembered her wedding to Primo Vasile. Even though they'd lied to her about the severity of her father's illness, she could not escape from Vasile's blackmail. If anything, it made it vital that she cooperate. If her father was going to regain his health and eventually leave hospital,

Vasile's threat to take incriminating evidence to the police became more meaningful.

Once again, it had seemed her life was horribly out of her own control and she would still be forced to submit to Vasile's blackmail.

Then Marco had launched his attack on her.

And suddenly her whole world had been thrown into a tailspin of an altogether different magnitude.

Just about everything Marco had said and done that afternoon had horrified her. She'd been subjected to a relentless bombardment of vicious accusations, unbelievable deceptions and harsh truths about the past.

But nothing had hurt as badly as the discovery that everything that had ever happened between them had been a lie. Marco had been deceiving her from day one.

Claudia shut her eyes and tried to close her mind too. Horrible thoughts were churning in her head, threatening to tear her apart from the inside. She couldn't let herself think about any of it yet. It was too raw. Too overwhelming.

She took several steadying breaths, opened her eyes and focused on the view outside the window, determined to keep calm.

A magnificent winter sunset filled the western sky, painting it a brilliant tangerine with wide contrasting ribbons of silver-grey cloud slicing through it. The sun was a blazing ball of fire at the centre, made all the more dramatic by the stark black silhouettes of winter trees in the foreground.

Suddenly her eyes filled with tears once more. Although she knew it was crazy, she wanted to talk to Marco about the sunset. She knew it was an irrational desire brought about by the memory of the relationship she'd once believed in—the relationship that had been a total sham—but that didn't make the longing to talk to Marco any less real.

They'd talked about anything and everything—she'd thought it was part of what had made them grow so close. He'd always understood what was on her mind, and never teased her when she wanted to talk about things other people might find silly.

Her discovery that Marco had been using her should have obliterated any positive feelings she had for him. Those feelings had been built on a web of deceit and should have come crumbling down when that web was destroyed.

Instead, she wanted to talk to him about the sunset, and she found herself longing to go back to when things between them had been good.

Why did her heart still yearn for him?

Why did she want to talk to him when he had hurt her so badly?

Because she was in love.

Her heart skipped a beat and she clutched her hands together on her lap. She was still in love with Marco. After everything that had happened, every horrible thing he had said and done to her, she still loved him.

She squeezed her eyes shut but she couldn't squeeze out the truth. Marco had set her up. Lied to her. Manipulated her in the worst possible way.

How could she still love him?

'Are you going to answer that?' Marco's voice cut through her thoughts and she suddenly realised her mobile phone was ringing.

She shook her head, trying to pull herself together, and drew the phone out of her bag. It was Francesca. Her stepmother had called repeatedly over the last few days, but after the first time Claudia had left her phone on silent, letting her voicemail pick up. She hadn't wanted to speak to the woman who was in cahoots with her blackmailer. She'd agreed to do what they'd asked of her—wasn't that enough?

But now there was something important she wanted to ask Francesca.

'Claudia, darling? Where are you?' Francesca's voice rang in her ears. 'Why haven't you returned my messages?'

'I told you that I'd be there. And then I left you a message confirming when and where we'd meet in the Caribbean,' Claudia said. 'There was nothing else to say. I already told you I didn't want to discuss the arrangements any more.'

'But there's so much to finalise. You haven't chosen your—'

'My father is not dying,' Claudia interrupted. 'Why did you lie to me?'

There was a deathly silence.

'What do you mean?' Francesca asked. It was the first time Claudia had ever heard her sound so uncertain.

'I was at the hospital today. The doctors explained everything—he'll be well enough to come home soon.'

'Yes, isn't it wonderful?' Francesca's voice was falsely high and enthusiastic. 'I was going to tell you the good news when I saw you in person—it's not the sort of thing to leave on voicemail.'

'Why not? It's good news,' Claudia asked.

'Of course it is,' Francesca said. 'We'll talk about it more when we meet up. But first there's the question of your dress, the flowers—'

'I'm not interested in any of that,' Claudia said shortly. 'You choose the dress.'

'But really, darling—'

Claudia snapped her phone shut, switched it off and tossed it back in her bag.

Her worst suspicions had been confirmed. Francesca had deliberately lied to her when she'd told her that Hector was dying. She lifted her hands and pressed them over her face, subconsciously trying to rub away the feelings of betrayal and loneliness that were swamping her.

She'd always known Francesca didn't love her, or even like her very much. But she'd never thought her capable of such a cruel, unthinkable thing. Who could lie about something like that? Who would even want to?

Claudia didn't think of herself as naïve, but now she realised that was exactly what she had been. Francesca and Vasile had obviously been planning to blackmail her for some time, and had concocted the story about her father's illness being terminal to give themselves extra leverage over her. How inconvenient it must have been for them when they'd discovered his health was improving.

She'd been naive with Marco too. Maybe not at first. But when he'd appeared in London, and then in Wales, she should have sent him packing.

But she couldn't dwell on that now. She still had to think about her father and what she could do to keep him safe from Vasile. If Marco really intended to keep her from the wedding, then she was in trouble. Or rather—her father was. Because then Vasile would carry out his threat, and take the evidence he had on her father to the police.

'Everything all right?' Marco asked blandly.

'Don't try to sound like you care,' Claudia said. 'I thought you were the one who was pleased we were finally being honest with each other.'

'You're right, I do appreciate honesty,' Marco said. 'I thought I detected some tension in your telephone conversation. I was curious what it was about.'

'That was my stepmother.' Claudia was beyond guarding what she said. 'She wants to know what dress I'll be wearing for the wedding. I told her to choose for me.'

'You do seem to have left that decision a little late,' Marco said. 'Will you be saying your vows on the beach at sunset?'

'You tell me,' Claudia snapped. 'You seem to know more than I do.'

'Details of the wedding and following celebrations are rather sketchy,' Marco said without expression. 'I can tell you the name of the official who is booked to perform the ceremony but, apart from that, not much. I suspect limited cash flow might be causing a problem.'

Claudia turned sideways to look at him. It was rapidly growing dark—the roadside was lined with trees, which blocked out the final rays of light from the western sky—but she could just about see his face.

'Why are you taking me to the Caribbean?' she asked.

'It's where you want to go,' he said. 'You've just told your stepmother you'll be there.'

'It's not where I *want* to go,' she said. 'And you told me you were not going to allow the wedding to go ahead—so why take me there?'

'You're right—it won't go ahead as planned,' he replied. 'But I want Vasile to see you with me. And I want you to see what happens to people who cross me.'

'I've already seen what you've done to me,' she said bitterly, thinking about how he'd lied to her and made her trust him. How he'd humiliated her with her desire for him, even after she'd found out the truth.

'No, you haven't,' he said. 'I'm nowhere near finished with you yet.'

A cold shiver prickled down her spine and she turned her head forward. The sports car was speeding along the country road, hungrily eating up the distance to the city. Soon they'd be on the motorway and she'd have barely any time left.

The last few days had been overwhelming for her and she no longer felt any confidence in her own judgement. But suddenly she found herself considering telling Marco about the blackmail.

What more harm could it do? She'd believed Marco when he'd told her that he would not allow the wedding to take place. But, if she didn't marry Vasile, he would turn her father in to the police. She couldn't let that happen—protecting her father was all she had to cling on to in the mess her life had become.

'It's not my choice to marry Primo Vasile,' she blurted.

'We always have a choice,' Marco said, keeping his eyes firmly on the road ahead.

'They're going to hurt my father if I don't do it,' she said.

'How?' Marco demanded, glancing at her with his piercing gaze. 'How are they going to hurt him?'

'I knew I shouldn't trust you!' Claudia cried, folding her arms across her chest and hugging herself tightly. 'You just want to know what it is they have on him, so that you can use it yourself!'

'I'm just interested,' Marco said. 'In all the years I've been following the situation, I've never found anything on your father. As far as I can tell, he's kept his nose clean.'

'*The situation*,' Claudia echoed. 'You are so cold! You are talking about my family.'

'Because of what they—you—did to *my* family,' he responded.

'I was thirteen years old when we came to Turin!' she gasped. 'When all this started.'

'You're an adult now,' Marco said. 'Responsible for your own actions. You make your own decisions.'

'I didn't just decide to marry Primo,' she said. 'I told you— they are blackmailing me. Threatening to hurt my father!'

'Blackmail—that's a serious accusation,' he said. 'Maybe I can add that to the catalogue of crimes I'll be using as evidence against Vasile. But I'll need to know the details.'

'I can't tell you. I'm scared you'll use the information against my father,' she said, dragging her fingers through her hair, which was still tangled from their lovemaking. 'And Primo *will* use it if I don't go through with the wedding,' she finished in dismay.

'So it's going to come out anyway,' Marco said. 'You might as well tell me now.'

She bit her lip and turned away to stare blindly out of the passenger window. She didn't know what to do, but she had to find some way to stop her father getting hurt.

Marco put the folder of documents back into his briefcase and looked across at Claudia. She was still sleeping, curled up under a blanket in the aeroplane seat. They were halfway into their private flight to the Caribbean and she had already been asleep for a couple of hours.

Marco was far too wired for sleep, despite the fact that he hadn't had much rest over the past few days. He'd been trying to read the documents detailing the evidence he'd compiled against Vasile and Francesca—it was almost impossible to believe that his family would finally be avenged. But his thoughts had been completely overtaken by Claudia.

He watched her sleeping. She was exquisite—more beautiful than when they'd first met four years ago. Maybe it was because she'd grown her fringe out and he could see the delicate arch of her brows and the smooth width of her forehead, but her stunning bone structure seemed to be even more defined. And her clear skin looked even more luminous, with the softest sheen like the finest silk.

He looked at the gentle arc of her dark lashes, and pictured the incredible colour of her eyes. It wasn't just the warm shade of golden brown that made them so arresting, it was the way they appeared to be lit from within, almost like tiger's eye gemstones, which seem to glow in layers, drawing the eye deep into the precious stone.

He imagined how gorgeous they would look in the Caribbean light, gazing lazily up at him as they lay together on the soft white sand, warm water lapping gently at their feet.

Suddenly the image shattered and he found himself picturing her distraught face after he'd confronted her with the truth in her father's study. The pain and betrayal in her eyes had pierced him like a jagged knife, tearing through his emotional barricades and slicing down to expose his nerves.

But he had been so wrapped up in his own agonising memories when he'd recounted what Vasile had done to his family that somehow Claudia's pain and distress had become indistinguishable from his own.

Now he let himself remember how horrified she had looked. How completely devastated she'd seemed at the discovery that he'd been using her all along.

A stab of conscience pricked at him.

He pushed it down ruthlessly.

He had wanted to hurt her. He had wanted her to share in the pain that had consumed him for twelve years. It couldn't have been that much of a surprise to her—she'd always known about his past, about the way their families were connected. It must have simply been frustration that her attempt to pretend ignorance of the past—to slip in past his defences again—had not succeeded.

He would not let her dupe him again. When they'd first met he'd made the mistake of letting down his guard and giving her the benefit of the doubt. That had nearly led to unthinkable consequences.

This time he'd thought that he'd been the one in control—that he'd been the one calling the shots. But now he realised she had started to get under his skin once again, drawing him into her world with her subtle emotional displays.

He'd felt her distress in Wales when she'd wept for her father, and he'd shared her joy when she'd discovered he wasn't dying. He'd even felt a jolt of protectiveness towards her as it had become clear that she had been deliberately misled.

He jerked to his feet and walked away down the plane, feeling his fingers coil round into tight fists.

The only thing he had to remember was how Claudia had deliberately taken him out of the country, allowing Vasile access to Bianca.

The background noise of the aeroplane engines roared in his ears. He looked at his watch, wishing the journey would be over soon. He hated flying, hated the confinement. Usually he passed the time by burying himself in his work. But he was too distracted to concentrate.

His thoughts turned to Claudia once again—this time to her assertion that Francesca and Vasile were blackmailing her into marriage. He realised that she was probably telling the truth. He believed that they'd lied to her about Hector's illness, and blackmail was well within Vasile's capabilities.

Another unwanted jolt of protectiveness towards Claudia made itself felt, but he ignored it. So what if Vasile was using her now? Four years ago she had been acting for Vasile when she'd set Bianca up.

He turned back and looked bitterly at Claudia—still lost in sleep. The only time in his adult life he'd ever slept soundly was during the few months he'd spent with her four years ago. He told himself that his relationship with her had made him soft, had made him let down his guard.

The possibility that he'd slept well because he was happy—*because being with Claudia made him happy*—drifted into his mind. He clenched his jaw shut and rammed the thought aside.

He wasn't wrong about her. And she was going to pay for what she'd done.

Claudia stood staring out across the emerald lagoon, hardly able to believe she was actually in the Caribbean, but the tropical sun was shining brightly, heating her body through the thin sarong she had wrapped over her bikini and the warm water was lapping gently at her bare feet. She could see silvery fish flashing past her in the crystal clear water close to the shore, and further out she could see the spectacular breakers where they crashed over the coral reef that surrounded the island, partially protecting the beach from the power of the ocean waves.

Marco had brought her to an exclusive private island resort

where they were staying in their own luxury villa in a grove of palm trees, on an idyllic bay reserved for their personal use. The island was close to St Lucia, which was where she had agreed to meet Vasile and Francesca, and Marco had said he would take her there at the right time, although he'd assured her again the wedding would not be going ahead.

'Beautiful, isn't it?'

Marco's voice beside her made her jump.

'Do you have to sneak up on me like that?' she said touchily, continuing to stare resolutely out across the lagoon.

'I didn't sneak,' he said. 'You were obviously lost in thought.'

'I was wondering how to get off this island,' she said. She still had to find a way to make him change his mind about letting her marry Primo—she couldn't let him carry out his threat to take the incriminating evidence about her father to the police. 'I don't like being your prisoner here. Why couldn't you have taken us to a normal hotel like normal people?'

'You're not my prisoner,' he said. 'You can leave any time you choose—just ask Pierre and he'll take you over to St Lucia. But I'm surprised you don't like it here. I thought you'd enjoy the isolation. Apart from reminding you of your grandmother, I thought that was the main attraction of the cottage in Wales.'

'Don't do that,' Claudia snapped.

'What?' Marco asked.

'Don't keep acting like you know me, like we're…friends or something.'

'I do know you. I made it my business to know you,' he said. 'And we've never been just friends.'

Something in the tone of his voice made a spark of electricity prickle across her skin and she turned to look at him.

She drew in an inadvertent breath of appreciation as she laid eyes on him—he truly was a magnificent man. He was only wearing his swimming trunks, and nothing was left to her imagination—not the impressive width of his shoulders and powerful biceps, or the well-defined muscles of his chest and stomach. His bronzed skin glowed with vitality in the warm sunlight, making her want to reach out and touch him, to feel the potent masculine energy that was flowing through his body.

She lifted her gaze to his face, determined not to let him catch her ogling him, but she was too late. His eyes bored into her with an intensity that let her know that he was well aware of her train of thought.

'Four years ago, before you left me, it felt like you were my friend,' she said, ignoring the way her pulse-rate had accelerated, and turned to look back out to sea.

'That was the whole point,' Marco said.

'The *whole* point?' She frowned and spun back to stare up him. 'I thought I was almost…incidental, part of your plan for revenge because I was involved with the people who hurt your family.'

'You were never incidental,' Marco said, lifting a hand to trace his fingertips lightly over her cheek.

'Don't.' She shrugged his hand away and took a step backwards, despite the way her body suddenly longed to lean into his.

'Do we have to go through this every time?' Marco asked, closing the distance between them and sliding one hand round her waist to pull her closer still. The heat from his powerful body burned through the delicate fabric of her sarong and she felt butterflies of anticipation flutter in her stomach.

But it was wrong. After everything that had happened

between them, it was wrong to fall into his arms again. She might have fallen in love with him, but if she had any self-respect she would push him away for good.

'No. I mean there won't be any more times,' she said, ignoring the heavy feeling of loss that settled inside her at the thought of never lying in Marco's arms again. 'Not now I know you are just using me.'

'We made love in Italy, after you knew the truth,' he said, slipping his other hand under the sarong to cup the curve of her bottom.

'That wasn't *love*,' Claudia said, suddenly finding the will to push him away and take another step backwards. As his hands lost contact with her she felt herself sway with intense disappointment—as if she had just lost some vital part of herself.

'No, it wasn't,' Marco agreed. 'You made your feelings for me plain afterwards when you said that you hated me. But that doesn't mean it wasn't good sex. Incredible sex.'

He stepped closer once more, his well-toned muscles rippling deliciously beneath his taut bronze skin, sorely testing her resolve to keep her distance. Although the soft sand shifted beneath his feet, he moved with an amazing fluid grace that spoke of power and control.

She gazed at his superb athletic form, bewildered by a haze of conflicting thoughts and emotions. When they'd first met, she'd believed that he was a good man—the kind of man who took care of people. In her heart she'd felt they had made a real connection, but he'd proven her wrong when he'd disappeared. And almost everything he'd done since then had been at odds with her initial belief in him.

'Is that all it ever was?' she asked. Could she really have fallen in love with someone so heartless? 'It felt like so much more.'

'It was an act,' he said. 'We were both acting.'

'It can't have been just an act,' she protested, not caring about saving face in front of him. She was losing—had lost—something that really mattered to her and she needed to come to terms with what had happened. 'The kindness you showed me, the way you seemed to understand what I was feeling and thinking about everything. You were inside my head and my heart.'

'I did my job well,' Marco said, looking down at her dispassionately, despite the tug of some unidentifiable emotion bubbling distractingly inside him. He ignored it—he would not let her get to him again. She was obviously getting desperate—playing another of her games with him. 'How do you think I got where I am today? When Vasile took everything my family owned I was left with next to nothing. I worked hard to build my business, but it takes more than commitment and effort. To be successful it's vital to understand what motivates people.'

'But that's not what you're like—I know it isn't.' Her eyes were wide as she stared up at him, and he felt his chest ache in a subconscious response to the innocent image she was projecting. She was trying to appeal to his better nature—but that was something that he'd slammed shut the day she'd betrayed Bianca. 'You're not the kind of man who uses people and takes what he wants without caring who gets hurt.'

'You don't know me,' he said, suddenly reaching out to drag her hard against him. 'Because this is exactly what I'm like.'

'No, I don't believe it. Let me go!' She struggled in his arms, trying to pull away, but he tightened his hold on her with one arm clamped around her waist and lifted his other hand to stroke her cheek.

'You don't want me to let you go,' Marco said, dipping his

head close to hers so that his mouth hovered only inches above hers. 'You want me to kiss you senseless. Then make love to you, right here on the sand.'

'That's the last thing I want.' She stopped struggling against him—it was simply making her dangerously aware of his raw masculine sensuality. She took a breath and stood absolutely still, trying to close her mind to the mental picture of making love with Marco on the beach and suppress the feelings that image aroused.

'Maybe that's what your head is telling you,' he said, stepping just far enough away from her to let his smouldering gaze slide lazily down from her head to her toes. 'But your body is telling you something completely different.'

'It's not my head speaking to me,' Claudia said, doing her best to ignore the physical sensation ignited by the sweep of his gaze. 'If I listened to my head I'd be on a boat out of here. It's my heart—in my heart I can't believe you are doing this.'

'You ought to be grateful to me,' Marco said. 'In two days' time Vasile will be destroyed and you'll be free of him.'

'But what about my father? If I don't marry him—'

'Vasile will go to prison whether you marry him or not,' Marco said. 'And if I let you go ahead with the wedding you would lose everything. Any funds transferred from your trust fund would be seized to repay Vasile's debts.'

'I don't care about money!' Claudia gasped. 'I was doing it to protect my father—to stop Primo revealing damaging information.'

'What does Vasile say he has on your father?' Marco asked.

'I'm not telling you!' Claudia said. 'You'll just use the information yourself.'

'I don't believe Vasile has anything,' Marco said. 'God knows I've invested enough time and money looking for incriminating evidence. Did they show you proof?'

Claudia bit her lip and looked up at Marco, thinking she'd be a fool to tell him anything. But she also knew that Marco was never going to let her marry Primo, so the information was going to come out anyway.

'He took money from the pension fund,' she said quietly. 'I don't know why he did it—he must have been intending to replace it, but then he got sick.'

A triumphant look flashed across Marco's face and Claudia stared up at him in agitation. She had the feeling that, yet again, he knew something she didn't.

'*Vasile* embezzled the pension fund, not your father,' Marco said. 'Millions of euros. Hard evidence of that was part of the information I picked up from my legal team in Turin.'

'I don't…' Claudia's voice died away in confusion. 'But *they* had evidence. Proof that my father had transferred money.'

'Did you study them properly?' Marco asked. 'Were they original documents?'

'I don't know…' Claudia stared at Marco momentarily stunned. She realised just how much of a fool she'd been. She'd let Primo and Francesca use her without properly questioning what they had told her.

She'd known her father wasn't guilty, but she'd been too scared to risk being wrong about it. They'd manipulated her perfectly—playing on her love for her father who, they'd told her, was dying. They knew that Claudia would never willingly let anything bad happen to her father. The whole situation had horrified her so much that she'd simply agreed to their demands.

'Oh, my God!' she said, covering her face with her hands. She'd let herself be used—had agreed to marry Vasile—and now Marco despised her for her weakness. 'I've been such a fool!'

Marco looked at Claudia, watching her realisation that she had been duped. The change that came over her was so profound that he had no doubt that it was genuine.

A brief, ironic smile flashed across his face as he thought about Vasile's desperate attempt to save himself from financial ruin. It amused Marco that Vasile clearly had no idea that money would not be anywhere near enough to save him.

But that moment of satisfaction was short-lived. As he stared at Claudia—face buried in her hands and shoulders huddled forward in misery—an unexpected surge of a different emotion churned in the pit of his stomach. He forced it down angrily—he would *not* let himself feel sorry for her. She deserved whatever she got.

He'd already suspected that she'd been the victim of Vasile and Francesca, but he'd felt no pity for her then. After all, she'd been the one doing their dirty work in the past, and it stood to reason that she knew how they operated. It was her own fault if she was foolish enough to be taken in by them. There was even a certain poetic justice to it. After all, she should pay for her part in what had happened to Bianca.

So why did her obvious distress affect him now?

He realised that she was shaking, despite the heat of the tropical sun. Was she crying? He didn't think so, but she was obviously experiencing a powerful reaction to the discovery that her stepmother and Vasile had played her for a fool.

Suddenly she dropped her hands and lifted her face to look

at him. Her face was startlingly pale and her golden-brown eyes seemed huge.

'Is it true?' she asked urgently. 'Is it true that my father is safe? That Francesca and Primo can't hurt him?'

'Yes,' Marco answered flatly, forcing down his automatic response to the appeal in those wide, innocent looking eyes.

'Oh, thank God!' she said. A spark of relief lit her face and a spot of colour returned to her cheeks. 'I've been so desperately worried about him.'

'You were very quick to believe him guilty,' Marco said, wondering how they had convinced her. As far as he was aware, Hector had led a spotless business life.

Claudia pressed her lips together, looking perplexed.

'I didn't believe it, not at first,' she said. 'But I just couldn't take the risk. Primo said he'd go straight to the police if I didn't do want he wanted. And Francesca backed him up.'

'Well, you'll be free of her soon,' Marco said dispassionately. 'She'll be going to jail too, for her part in Vasile's schemes.'

'Oh, my poor father,' Claudia gasped. 'How awful to have his wife arrested and sent to prison.'

'He should thank me,' Marco said. 'For freeing him of that bloodsucking leech. Marrying her was the worst mistake he ever made.'

'You heartless pig!' Claudia exclaimed, looking at his cold, hard face.

'Don't you wish he'd never replaced your mother with that witch?' Marco asked.

Claudia stared at Marco in shock. She'd wished a million times that she still had her mother—but as far as she was concerned, Francesca wasn't a replacement for her. And she knew her father didn't view her like that either. Until her grandma had died he had taken her to Wales as often as he could, keeping up her only connection with her real mother.

'Francesca wasn't a replacement,' she said. 'My father never tried to make her that—and, goodness knows, Francesca didn't try to act like a mother.'

'Just think how much better your life would have been without her,' Marco pressed. 'And, more importantly, Primo Vasile would never have been part of it.'

'I never liked Primo. And I always had the feeling my father didn't either. Although he'd be shocked to discover just how evil Primo has been.' she said. 'But when he married Francesca she was already his business partner, so my father chose to let that be.'

'Another almost fatal mistake,' Marco said. 'He will be pleased to see Vasile rot in prison.'

'Not everyone is as cold and brutal as you,' she said. 'Just because Primo makes my skin crawl, doesn't mean I want to see him suffer.'

'Even after what he's done to you?'

She looked at him, startled by how fierce he seemed, but then there was always a look of barely restrained fury in his eyes when he mentioned Primo Vasile.

'I don't know—it will take a while to get used to,' she said. 'He does deserve to be punished, but you seem to take such unholy pleasure in bringing him down. And anyone associated with him.'

'Not *everyone* associated with him,' Marco said, his eyes boring into her, dark and unrelenting in their scrutiny. 'Just anyone who hurt my family.'

Suddenly she felt a terrible jolt of cold hostility firing into her. The realisation that Marco's absolute hatred of Vasile

extended to her struck like a cataclysmic bolt of lightning out
of a clear blue sky. She staggered back a step, feeling a con-
tinuous wave of enmity battering her down.

'What did *I* ever do to make you hate me so much?' she
cried. 'I never did anything to hurt you or your family.'

It was unbearable that he despised her so much. She'd
thought he was against her simply because of her family and
the fact that he'd discovered she was marrying Primo Vasile.

But she knew now that, for some reason, it was more than
that—it was personal.

'You hurt me in the worst possible way,' Marco bit out,
'when you tried to hurt my sister.'

'What?' Claudia exclaimed. 'I never did anything to
Bianca! She was my friend and I would never, ever have done
anything to hurt her.'

'But you had no qualms about leading her into Vasile's lair.'

'I don't know what you are talking about,' she cried,
twisting her hands in front of her. 'There must have been a
terrible misunderstanding.'

'There was no misunderstanding,' Marco said. 'You set
Bianca up—invited her to a party where you told her you
would introduce her to contacts in the fashion industry. Then
you left her to go to the event on her own, where she would
be easy prey for Vasile.'

'I remember the party,' Claudia said. 'We didn't go with
her in the end because—'

'You got me out of the way,' Marco interrupted. 'Because
you took me out of the country where I wouldn't be able to
protect my sister from Vasile.'

'Why did she need protecting from Primo?' Claudia
demanded. 'It was just a party at a new restaurant. It never

occurred to me that she wouldn't be fine—she went with mutual friends.'

'Friends who had no idea to keep her away from a man called Primo Vasile,' Marco said.

'I know you hate him,' Claudia said. 'I understand that now. But what would he do to Bianca?'

'He got her drunk.' The intense emotion throbbing in Marco's voice sliced right through her, making her share the agony he was feeling. 'Possibly he even gave her drugs to weaken her inhibitions.'

'Oh, my God!' Claudia clamped her hand over her mouth in horror. 'What happened? Was she all right?'

'How dare you ask that?' Marco seized her arms and glared down at her—the fury emanating from him making the air crackle around them. 'You're the one who led her into the jaws of that shark!'

'What happened. Please tell me she was all right.' Claudia felt tears prick in her eyes as she thought about Bianca.

'He tried to get information about me and my business dealings out of her,' Marco said, his fingers biting into Claudia's upper arms as he spoke. 'Then he tried to leave with her.'

'Tried?' Claudia whispered, desperate to hear that no lasting harm had come to Bianca. She hardly dared to breathe as she stared up into Marco's livid face.

'A friend of mine saw them together,' Marco grated. 'He was at the party quite by chance, but every day I thank God he was there.'

'Your friend looked after her?' Claudia asked, feeling tears of relief spill from her eyes. She was mortified to know that her invitation to that party had led, however inadvertently, to Bianca getting hurt.

'Weeping won't make up for what you did.' Marco's fingers tightened on her arm momentarily. Then he pushed her savagely aside, a look of pure disgust on his face. 'You preyed on an innocent girl who thought you were her friend.'

Claudia stumbled and by the time she'd caught her breath Marco was gone, surging out into the deeper water with long powerful strokes.

CHAPTER ELEVEN

CLAUDIA stood at one of the elegant ceiling to floor windows, watching for Marco's return. It was several hours since their argument on the beach and during that time she had showered and put on a fresh dress. Now she was waiting.

The view was divine, although she was hardly in the mood to enjoy it. It wasn't surprising that the designer of the sumptuous vacation villa had included three enormous ocean view windows in the main living area. Each one was dressed with long pure white curtains that rippled in the breeze coming off the water, and each one framed a vista that was simply stunning.

Marco had brought her to a tropical paradise.

It was a million miles away from the cottage in Wales, in every respect. To start with, it felt as if the whole cottage could have easily fitted inside just that one luxurious room of the villa. And the view outside was equally far removed from Wales. The powder-white coral sand was the opposite of the black rocks and dark grey limestone of the Pembrokeshire coast. And the mirror-like emerald water was totally different from the churning slate grey sea that had nearly cut her off with the incoming tide.

It was almost impossible to believe that it was only a few

days since she'd arrived in Pembrokeshire and gone down to the stormy beach to test out that digital camera. So much had happened. So many awful truths had been revealed.

But Marco's latest accusation had left her reeling.

She could not process the discovery that he believed she had deliberately done something to hurt Bianca. Even the idea that she could do such a thing made her feel sick. That Marco thought it was possible, even after they had spent so much time together, shocked her to the core.

She'd thought that he understood her—that in a short time he had come to know her better than anybody else had ever known her. She'd thought that they were soul mates.

She couldn't have been more wrong.

She had fallen in love with someone who didn't know her at all. Someone who despised her.

Marco powered through the calm water of the lagoon, trying to work off some of the anger that gripped his body, but it was taking him a long time to feel any better. The glow of exercise fatigue in his muscles started to seem like an unattainable goal—his body was too full of raging energy that needed to be released so he just kept swimming back and forth across the bay.

He had chosen to stay in a sheltered cove where the tranquil water would be ideal for bathing and making love to Claudia. Now he wished he'd chosen somewhere known for rolling surf. He could do with the physical challenge of battling the elemental force of the water.

Finally he headed in to the beach and stood staring back out to where the breakers foamed across the reef, letting the sun dry his body. There was a hollow irony in the fact that he'd selected this location with Claudia in mind—and it wasn't lost on him. Somehow he had let himself imagine that nothing would have changed between them, that this would be a continuation of their time in the cottage in Wales.

He was an utter fool.

He'd planned to seduce Claudia, make her open up her heart to him, then toss her brutally aside when he had no more use for her.

He'd done that. Everything had gone according to plan. So why was he hammering out his fury in the ocean, trying to swim himself towards exhaustion, rather than enjoying the triumph of this moment?

The distraught expression on Claudia's face when he'd pushed her away from him flashed through his mind. He'd been so furious that he knew he'd used considerable force. Had she fallen? He'd never looked back to see.

He clenched his fists and exhaled heavily. Why should he care if she'd fallen? The sand was soft—she would not have been injured.

Besides, the whole point of his plan was to hurt her. He wanted her to feel the way he'd felt, back when *he'd* realised *she'd* duped him. Four years ago he'd gone in with his eyes open, knowing exactly who she was, and yet somehow he'd fallen for her charms. He'd lowered his defences, letting her play with his common sense and duty to protect his sister. Then she had sent Bianca right into Vasile's grasp.

Now that the situation was out in the open should not—*would not*—make any difference to what he did or the way he felt. He'd made up his mind about Claudia long ago and judged her accordingly. He'd set his course and he'd followed it. And he would continue to see it through.

He would not tolerate her messing with his head again.

making him question himself. Nothing had changed. Claudia was still as treacherous as his mother and had betrayed them in the same poisonous way. Bianca had been at the mercy of Vasile that night, and it was only the fortuitous intervention of Marco's friend that had saved her.

By the time Claudia saw Marco walking back up the beach to the villa her mood had completely changed. When she'd first discovered the root cause of his hostility towards her she had been totally shocked. She'd felt sick to her stomach that he could genuinely have believed such awful things about her.

Now a very different emotion was coiling through her, raising her heart rate and creating tension in every single inch of her body.

Anger.

Marco had treated her appallingly. Not only now, but also back when he'd first met her. Every moment of every hour they had spent together had been a lie. He had just been waiting for her to trip up—all the time believing that she was a terrible person. And he had never, ever given her the chance to defend herself.

She heard his steps on the wide wooden veranda and turned to watch him come in through the open door.

'Still here?' The sarcastic tone in his voice grated across her nerve endings, tightening all her muscles to a whole new level of tension. 'I half expected you'd be gone.'

'You brought me here,' she snapped. 'I thought this was where you wanted me. Or have you grown tired of your little game?'

She stared across the room at him angrily, noticing a fine dusting of white sand on the bronzed skin of his chest. His hair was still slightly damp and was stiff and spiky with sea salt.

'Yes,' he said. 'I am growing tired of your presence, but un
fortunately I haven't finished with you yet. There is still one
more thing to do.'

'You mean you want to flaunt me in front of Primo Vasile?'
she demanded, planting her hands on her hips. 'Like some
kind of trophy.'

'Something like that,' Marco said.

'You are disgusting,' she said furiously. 'I wish I'd never
met you. There is no way I'll be part of your scheme.'

'I'll drag you there with me.' Marco looked at her through
dangerously narrowed eyes. 'Kicking and screaming if need be.'

'I *will* be kicking and screaming—and worse,' Claudia
replied, not letting herself be affected by the threat in his
words. 'You just try to take me somewhere else against my
will, and you'll find out how hard I'll fight you.'

'What a relief that you are finally showing your true
colours,' Marco said, walking menacingly across the room
towards her. 'Rather like a cornered rat.'

'No—but that's just it.' Claudia stood her ground and squared
her shoulders to him. 'You never let me show my true colours.'

'I was waiting to see what you'd do,' Marco said. He was
standing so close to her that she could feel his hot breath on
her face, but he made no move to touch her. 'I was simply
giving you enough rope to hang yourself—I wanted to be
there to enjoy that moment.'

'You judged me by your own depraved standards!' Claudia
cried, raking her hands roughly through her hair to pull it back
from her flushed face. 'For no good reason whatsoever, you
simply assumed I was capable of the same disgusting behaviour that you are.'

'I had a good reason,' Marco said through gritted teeth.

'No. You didn't.' Claudia took a step closer to him and glared up into his face. 'You dragged me maliciously into your sick vendetta because that was what *you* wanted. And you never allowed me the simple courtesy of defending myself against crimes I didn't even know you believed me guilty of.'

'What courtesy did Vasile give my family?' Marco demanded. 'Did he ask my father's permission to seduce my mother into betraying him?'

'That's horrible,' Claudia said. 'But it has nothing to do with me.'

'You've been involved with him,' Marco accused.

'No, I haven't,' Claudia declared. 'Until a few days ago I hardly gave him any thought. I had no idea what he was like.'

'Of course you knew,' Marco said. 'You told me he made your skin crawl.'

'Just because I didn't take to him on the few occasions I met him does not mean I knew what terrible things he was capable of,' she said. 'And Bianca didn't know what he was like either.'

'Don't you dare bring Bianca into this,' Marco said angrily.

'Why shouldn't I? This all started with Bianca.' Claudia was picking up speed and there was no way she was going to let Marco dictate what she could and couldn't talk about. 'If you'd ever told her to watch out for Primo Vasile, she wouldn't have been so vulnerable to him. She would never have talked to him or accepted a drink from him.'

'Don't tell me how to look after my sister,' Marco grated. A surge of cold fury powered through him as he looked at Claudia. She would regret using his sister to argue against him.

'Why not? You did a lousy job of it,' she said. 'You were so arrogant you assumed your protection of her was all encompassing. You tried to control her life—but instead you took her away from a true friend and kept her ignorant of a genuine threat to her safety.'

'She would never have encountered Vasile if you hadn't invited her to that party,' Marco said. 'She didn't need to know about him and the level of depravity he stooped to when he destroyed our family.'

He glared at Claudia. How did she have the audacity to stand there and accuse him of failing his sister? She was the one who had done wrong. She was the betrayer—the snake in the grass.

'Not when she was a child, I agree,' Claudia said. 'But, although she was still young when we met, she was a grown woman. There was every chance she was going to come across Vasile at some point.'

'Not without a helping hand from you,' Marco said, but a nasty stab of doubt pricked him.

Claudia was wrong. She had to be. He would have done everything to keep Bianca safe—she hadn't needed to have her innocence sullied by knowledge of Vasile.

Except he hadn't kept her safe. That harsh, uncompromising truth thrust itself into the front of his mind.

'I knew nothing about it,' Claudia said. 'But a few days in your company and I'm starting to see how people like you and Vasile operate. I admit it's perfectly feasible that somehow Vasile was tracking my friends and contacts. Maybe it was even Francesca who took me to the first event where I met Bianca. I don't remember and it doesn't matter.' She took a breath and carried on. 'If you were even halfway decent you would have genuinely given me the benefit of the doubt and talked to me. And I promise I would never have let Bianca come anywhere near Primo Vasile.'

'Don't compare me to a bastard like Vasile,' Marco said, anger making his voice hard. 'He is nothing but filth. The lowest sort of scum on this earth.'

'You're exactly the same,' Claudia retorted. 'You've been blinded by hate—it's turned into an obsession. You're so hell bent on revenge that you've lost any sense of right and wrong.'

'I'm not like him.' Marco rejected the idea furiously. 'I would never do what he has done.'

'You've already done it,' Claudia cried. 'You are guilty of all the same crimes.'

'No,' Marco said, suddenly gripping her arms with his hands. His blood was raging through his body, making him tremble with anger. She was going too far.

'You seduced me, just like he seduced your mother,' Claudia said. 'All with the intention of destroying me and my family, the way he destroyed yours.'

'It was not the same thing,' Marco said, tightening his fingers on her arms to emphasize his words.

His head was throbbing, making it hard to think straight. But he knew she must be wrong.

'It doesn't matter what you say.' Claudia stepped backwards, jerking out of his grip. 'Whichever way you present it, it comes to the same thing. You are completely heartless.'

Suddenly a terrible expression passed across her face—a look of disgust combined with total devastation. Then, as if she was unable to bear another second with him, she turned and walked jerkily away.

He stood frozen to the spot, unable to make himself move

to try and stop her. Then, just as she reached the door, she turned back and spoke.

'Your hatred of Vasile has completely consumed you,' she said. 'And now, whether you admit it or not, you've become the man you hate.'

CHAPTER TWELVE

CLAUDIA flung herself across the veranda and staggered on to the sand, choking back the torrent of tears that was threatening to burst out of her. She would not cry in front of Marco. She would not cry until she was out of his sight.

She ran across the beach towards the sea, stumbling as the soft sand shifted beneath her feet, and finally sank down to her knees at the water's edge, sobbing her heart out.

By that point she was beyond caring whether Marco could see her. She was beyond coherent thought. The anger that had fuelled her only moments before had completely evaporated, leaving behind a desolate shadow of the woman who had defended herself so passionately, fearlessly standing up to Marco and calling him out on his appalling actions.

All that was left of her was a helpless wretch, huddled alone on the beach, weeping in solitary misery.

She felt horribly bereft. It was as if she had lost someone profoundly important to her—yet she knew she was grieving for something she'd never really had. Nothing had been real.

It had all been a lie.

* * *

Marco watched Claudia stumble across the beach, gripped by a maelstrom of raging emotions. As she collapsed beside the water he realised at once that she was weeping. Suddenly the fury that stormed within him was extinguished, and something deep inside him contracted painfully.

Claudia had said he had no heart—but she was wrong.

He could feel it breaking as he watched her weep.

At that moment he knew with absolute certainty that every word she had ever told him was true. And that he had taken her trust, the innermost secrets of her soul, and he'd used them against her in the worst possible way. He'd manipulated her and abused her trust. He'd chewed her up and spat her back out.

Her final words—*you've become the man you hate*—echoed agonisingly inside his mind.

The idea that he had turned into a monster like Vasile was utterly abhorrent—yet the truth in her accusation lacerated his soul. She had been right when she'd told him that his need for revenge had blinded him to what was true.

All along something inside him—which he'd forced right to the back of his consciousness—had recognised the signs of her innocence. His heart had known the truth, but his mind, filled with hatred and the obsessive need to avenge his family, had overpowered that truth. The anger that had driven him since his mother's betrayal had consumed him and he had chosen how to interpret everything Claudia had ever said or done, according to his own warped agenda.

When she'd told him that Vasile and Francesca were blackmailing her into marriage, he had believed her. In fact, he'd even felt a flash of concern for Claudia. But he had chosen to brutally suppress it, because it didn't fit in with his preconceived ideas about her. Instead he had concentrated on the cold satisfaction he'd felt, knowing that Vasile was desperate enough to do such a reckless thing.

Nothing had added up, but he had ploughed on regardless—too arrogant to re-evaluate.

Too scared to expose the chink in his heart.

A thunderbolt of understanding hit him square in the chest, making his heart thud and his eyes widen as he stared across the beach at Claudia.

He'd been too scared to expose his heart to her for one simple reason.

He was in love with her.

He'd been in love with her since the summer when they'd first met.

But she was the daughter of his enemy's partner. She'd been living in the home that should have been his. It had been impossible for him to admit those feelings—even to himself.

But, despite his constant denial, his feelings were real. That was why he'd spent so much time with her and why he had trusted Bianca with her, even though there'd been a niggle at the back of his mind telling him that he should keep his sister away from anyone even remotely connected to Vasile.

When Bianca had fallen into danger, he had to blame someone. He couldn't bear to admit that his love for Claudia had made him careless with his sister's safety. That he'd let her go unaccompanied to that party so that he could spend a blissful weekend alone with his lover.

He'd reacted instinctively, falling back on past prejudices and misconceptions. When his friend had called from Turin that night to tell him what had happened, it had been easier to blame Claudia. He'd lowered his guard and he couldn't stand feeling exposed. Even the mere possibility that Claudia had played him was intolerable—so he had clamped his heart shut and left.

Now he looked at her through the frame of swaying palm trees that surrounded the villa and he cursed himself.

All along she'd been open and honest with him, trusting him with treasured memories and secrets that were deeply meaningful to her. The young woman who spoke with such heartfelt emotion about the loss of her mother, about her beloved grandmother teaching her to bake and about her distress over her father's illness could never have been guilty of the things Marco had blamed her for.

Suddenly Marco felt his eyes filling with moisture.

He blinked in surprise and put his hand up to touch his face. It was wet with tears.

He never wept. Not even the night when his father had died and he'd discovered what Vasile had done to his family. That night he had barricaded his heart and filled his head with plans for revenge.

But now, somehow, Claudia had penetrated the ice packed around his heart. His defences had crumbled away, leaving him open and exposed. He was feeling her pain as sharply as if it were his own.

He couldn't bear to think of Claudia suffering, but her pain was all his fault. He longed to run across the beach to her, enfold her in his arms, tell her how sorry he was and beg for her forgiveness.

But that wouldn't erase all the agony he had caused. And he knew she wouldn't believe him. He had lied to her too much for her to believe him now.

He rubbed the back of his hand roughly across his face and dragged his eyes away from the window. Watching her sitting on the beach wouldn't help. He had to find a way to make things better. He had to find a way to prove he loved her.

The next morning Claudia stood on the powder-soft sand, letting the crystal clear water lap gently over her feet. She was slowly sinking. With every suck and pull of the waves the white sand shifted slightly until it was covering her feet, almost up to her ankles.

She couldn't seem to move. She just didn't have the energy.

She'd spent a sleepless night all alone in the magnificent four-poster bed, staring miserably at the sumptuous silken fabrics that draped tastefully around her, thinking about Marco and all the times they had spent together.

It was so hard to believe that it had been meaningless, but she had to accept it. She ought to leave—she didn't think Marco would try to stop her—but somehow she just couldn't. She'd never felt so desolate in her entire life.

Very late that evening she was due to meet Francesca and Vasile for the wedding—it was strange to think that right at that moment they were somewhere over the Atlantic, flying unawares into Marco's trap. Presumably that was what had kept him busy all night, talking on his mobile phone, tapping emails into his laptop computer.

She could have called them, warned them of Marco's intentions, but she believed he was telling the truth about their illegal activities. They had definitely tried to blackmail her, by lying about her father's health and falsely accusing him of theft. However, although she wouldn't try to stop Marco, she had no intention of going with him to be present when he challenged them. She wasn't interested in that. She just wanted to fly home and be with her father.

She knew he would be all right if Francesca went to prison. They had been living virtually separate lives for years. Claudia suspected that if her father wasn't so kind hearted he would have divorced her a long time ago.

A sound coming from behind her drew her out of her thoughts and she glanced over her shoulder to see Marco only a few feet away. He was coming towards her across the beach, looking absolutely awful. A sharp jab of concern for him went through her as she took in the pained expression on his face. There were dark circles under his haunted eyes and his jaw was shadowed black where he hadn't taken the time to shave.

'Are you all right?' She spoke instinctively, momentarily forgetting that she wasn't supposed to care whether he was all right or not. She tried to turn to face him, but her feet were still buried under the sand and she stumbled.

Marco was at her side in an instant, gently holding her steady. For a moment she thought he was going to pull her into his embrace—that was what she longed for him to do— but then, once he was certain she had regained her balance, he let go of her and stepped away.

Her heart sank, although she told herself she was stupid to even think about Marco embracing her ever again.

'My feet got stuck.' She said the first thing that came to her mind and lifted her gaze to meet his. 'You look awful,' she added. 'What happened? Has something gone wrong with your plan?'

'*Everything* was wrong with my plan,' Marco said. 'It was my plan that made me hurt you so badly.'

Claudia frowned up at him, letting his dark eyes delve deep into her eyes for the longest moment. He looked sincere. But, despite the small spark of hope that ignited within her, that maybe he'd realised that he'd been wrong about her, she had to be cautious.

'I'm sorry,' he said. 'I am sorry for everything—I've been so wrong. I am entirely to blame.'

'It's not your fault that Primo and Francesca tried to blackmail me,' Claudia replied, trying to keep her emotions steady. She didn't know where Marco was going with this unexpected apology but she had no reason to trust him. She'd done that in Wales, even knowing how he'd left her so coldly four years earlier, and it had brought her nothing but distress.

That wasn't entirely true, a tiny voice inside her head insisted. She'd been happy that evening in Wales. He'd brought her comfort, despite the fact that he was working towards his own goals. And he'd taken her to Turin and discovered that her father was not terminally ill.

'It *was* my fault,' Marco said. 'I could have ruined Vasile years ago—then he couldn't have touched you. But that wasn't enough for me. I wanted to hound him and make him suffer. I pressurized him intentionally, hoping he would be forced to take desperate measures that would give me something good to use against him. That was what drove him to embezzlement and finally to blackmail.'

Claudia stared at Marco, a bewildering array of thoughts and emotions bombarding her.

'I'd tear out my heart and give it to you,' Marco said, suddenly catching hold of her hands and holding them close to his chest. 'I'd do it in a heartbeat if it would help to make you feel even the slightest bit better.'

'I don't want that,' Claudia said. 'How would your suffering help me?'

'I'm sorry for everything I did,' he said again. 'I know

that will be hard for you to believe, after everything I've done to hurt you.'

'I want to believe you,' Claudia whispered, looking up at him. The emotional distress he was feeling was evident in his tortured expression, and she pulled her fingers out of his grasp to reach up and cup his face with her palm. His skin was warm and his stubble rough against her palm.

For a moment he closed his eyes and leant his cheek into her caress. Then, almost as if he couldn't allow himself even that small amount of comfort, he tipped his head away and looked at her.

'I wanted to do something—give you something—to prove I mean what I say,' Marco said. 'At first I couldn't think of anything. There is nothing that could ever be enough. I can never make up for what I did.'

'You don't have to do anything,' Claudia said. 'I believe you're sorry.'

And it was true. Somehow, deep inside, she knew he was sincere.

But she didn't want his apology. She didn't want his suffering.

She wanted him to love her—like she loved him.

'Come inside with me,' Marco said, taking her by the hand and leading her up the beach to the villa.

When they reached the doorway Claudia stopped in her tracks and stared into the huge living room in surprise. She had gone down to the sea through the bedroom door that morning and hadn't seen what Marco had done in the living room. No wonder she had heard him moving about half the night.

'It's beautiful,' Claudia said, letting her gaze run over the gorgeous Christmas decorations that adorned the entire room. There was even a Christmas tree standing tall and proud by one of the elegant windows, sparkling with multi-coloured lights.

'No, not that,' Marco said, leading her into the room and pulling her down on to the sofa beside him. 'Well, yes, I did decorate for you. But this is what I want you to see.'

He opened his laptop computer and clicked open a news channel website.

Claudia watched, confused at first, but she quickly realised what she was seeing.

'This is a news clip of Primo Vasile and Francesca Hazelton being arrested at Turin airport and taken into police custody,' Marco said, as if he needed to be sure she understood.

'But…' Claudia turned to him uncertainly.

'The police received compelling evidence against them,' Marco said. 'And the news crew were also tipped off about it. I doubt it has made international news channels, but I wanted you to be able to see proof of what has happened.'

'But I thought you wanted to be there, to let him know it was you who brought him down,' Claudia said, leaning forward to click on the video clip again. She couldn't quite believe what she was seeing.

Marco let her watch it through once more, then closed the laptop.

'Yes, I wanted to be there to humiliate him, as he humiliated my father. To let him know I was the one responsible for his destruction.'

He broke off and took a shuddering breath, appalled to think that for his whole adult life he had been driven by the need to seek vicious revenge on Vasile. But although Claudia had suffered too, she had no desire for retaliation. She didn't wish to see them suffer in return. There wasn't a vindictive bone in her body.

That thought had haunted him all night. And it had shamed him.

He turned to her urgently, catching her eye to really emphasise what he was about to say.

'I thought that being there in person to bring down Vasile was the thing that mattered to me most. But I found out I was wrong.'

'How? What changed your mind?' Claudia asked

'You.'

'Me?' Claudia frowned at him. 'You mean you gave it up for me? You've worked towards that moment for years.'

'It was meaningless,' Marco said. 'Compared to how I feel about you, it was utterly meaningless.'

She looked at him, hardly daring to breathe. Or to hope.

'I achieved what I set out to do. I deceived you. I made you care for me. And I think I broke your heart,' Marco said. 'But I also broke my own.'

He stood up and strode to the window and Claudia realised he was in the grip of very powerful emotions. She waited quietly, trying not to let the glimmer of hope that was building inside her grow too strong too soon. He'd said he'd broken his own heart. But she wouldn't let herself think about what that might mean.

'When Bianca first told me you were her new friend I was suspicious,' Marco continued. 'But when I met you I was overwhelmed.'

'I was overwhelmed by you too,' Claudia said, remembering how she'd been so impressed by him, so in awe of his incredible good looks and so flattered by his attention.

'You were beautiful, charming and wonderfully enthusiastic about life,' Marco said. 'I fell in love with you immediately.'

Claudia gasped, then covered her mouth with her hand, looking up at him with wide startled eyes. He'd said he'd fallen in love with her. But he'd used the past tense—he was talking about what happened more than four years ago.

'I know what you're thinking,' Marco said, gazing down at her shocked face. She looked so pale and vulnerable that he wanted to wrap her in his arms and protect her from the world.

The unbearable knowledge that *he* was the one she needed protection from lashed at him viciously, ripping through him—making his heart bleed in an agony of guilt-ridden sorrow.

'What?' she asked, her voice shaking.

'If I loved you—how could I have treated you so badly?'

He'd asked himself that question a million times since their terrible argument the night before. He hadn't been able to get it out of his mind. He truly must be a terrible person. A man as despicable as Primo Vasile.

'You were right when you said my hatred of Vasile blinded me,' he continued doggedly. 'That's why I never challenged you about our mutual connection to him. I told myself I was waiting to see what you'd do, to see if you'd reveal any involvement with him. The truth was I enjoyed your company too much to do anything that might make me lose you.'

He paused and drew in a long shaky breath.

'I wish you'd asked me about it.' Claudia gazed up into his haunted eyes. His suffering was drawn on every plane and angle of his face, and her heart contracted with the need to comfort him somehow. But she instinctively understood that he needed to complete his confession.

'So do I,' Marco said, pacing across to the window and back again.

'I still can't believe that all along you thought I knew what Primo did to your family,' she said. 'That you thought I was hiding that knowledge from you for some reason.'

'That's because you have a kind, pure heart,' Marco said, raking his hands in agitation through his already dishevelled hair. 'I know now that you would never be capable of such deception—but, as you said last night, I judged you by my own despicable standards.'

'Your family had been destroyed by Primo,' Claudia said, desperate to ease his pain. 'No wonder you were cautious.'

'I wasn't cautious. I was obsessed,' Marco said. 'I told myself I was giving you the benefit of the doubt. But I realise now that my hatred of your family was so strong that I was just waiting for you to trip up.'

He stopped pacing and looked down at her, making eye contact.

'I'd fallen in love with you—that's why it hurt me so much when I thought you had betrayed me,' he said.

'So you wanted to hurt me in return.' Claudia's voice was so quiet she could hardly hear it herself.

'I feel so ashamed,' he said, suddenly dropping down to his knees in front of her and taking her hands in his. 'How could I want to hurt the person I love?'

Claudia gazed into his eyes and saw they were clouded by a miasma of guilt and pain. But beneath that misery, she could see a glimmer of something else.

No, it was more than a glimmer. It was a warm bright glow and it was shining directly into her soul.

It was love. He loved her.

'I can never forgive myself for hurting you so badly,' Marco said.

'You must forgive yourself,' Claudia said, squeezing his large powerful hands with her own. 'Because *I* forgive you.'

'Why?' he asked. 'How can you? After every awful thing I've said and done?'

'Because I love you.'

She smiled, feeling the words sparkle in the air between them like a spell. It felt so good to say it—it was the truth from the very bottom of her heart—and at that moment she knew everything would be all right.

'But I broke your heart.'

From the bemused frown on Marco's face, she could tell he needed more convincing. She lifted her hand and smoothed it tenderly across the lines that creased his forehead.

'It isn't broken any more—feel it beating.' She took his hand and pressed it over her left breast. 'And with every beat my happiness is growing—my love for you is growing'

'You still want to be with me?' His voice was incredulous, but she could finally hear a tentative note of joy.

'Of course—I love you.'

'I love *you*.' He said the words solemnly, looking deep into her eyes, as if he still didn't think she would believe him.

'I've always loved you,' she said. 'I thought we were soul mates—I've never met anyone who understands me like you do.'

'But look how I used that understanding,' he said, a pang of guilt echoing through his voice.

'Shh,' she said, pressing her index finger lightly over his lips. They felt warm and vital under her fingertip. 'We don't need to think about it ever again. Primo and Francesca are going to prison—they're out of our lives for good.'

'That news clip I showed you was recorded hours ago,'

Marco said. 'They were arrested hours ago—but I felt nothing. In the end it meant nothing compared to my feelings for you.'

'Does Primo know he was arrested because of you?' she asked. Despite her conviction that they needed to put the past behind them, there were still one or two more things that needed to be said.

'No, I don't think so. And I don't care any more,' Marco replied, suddenly moving up to sit beside her on the sofa. 'When it comes to trial I may have to give evidence, but I don't care if he never knows it was me.'

'What will happen about the stolen money?' she asked. 'Will the people still lose their pensions?'

He cupped her face in his hands and leant forward to kiss her lips with aching tenderness.

'You are such a wonderful, kind person,' he murmured. 'Even with everything that's going on, you are thinking about other people. Don't worry. They will be all right. When all of Vasile's assets are seized, there will be enough money.'

'I'm glad,' Claudia said. 'I hated thinking about letting all those people down so badly.'

'You are an angel,' Marco said, kissing her again. 'Your goodness has freed me from my soul-destroying obsession to avenge my family. I love you more than I can ever say.'

Claudia slipped her arms around him and held him tight, watching the Christmas tree lights splinter into a kaleido-scope of colours reflected in the tears of happiness that suddenly filled her eyes.

She clung to him, never wanting to let him go, basking in the certain knowledge that he felt the same way.

'There's something else I need to tell you,' Marco said. 'I've sent a top antique restorer to the house in Piedmont. Your father's desk has been repaired. Only someone with an expert eye would be able to tell it had been damaged.'

'Thank you,' Claudia said, deeply touched by his thoughtfulness.

'It was the least I could do,' Marco replied quietly.

They were silent for a moment and Claudia looked around the room, noticing the decorations properly for the first time.

'You've brought Christmas to us early,' she murmured. Then she saw a delicious looking array of food had been set up on the side table—bright tropical fruit and Caribbean delicacies. 'And what's that wonderful smell?'

'Spiced rum punch,' he said. 'It seemed more suitable for the Caribbean than mulled wine.'

'For breakfast?' she said laughing.

'I wasn't thinking straight.' He smiled, looking almost bashful—if that was possible for such a heart-stoppingly gorgeous specimen of masculine perfection. 'There's plain juice if you prefer—or I can call for anything else you'd like.'

'No—' she laughed '—I want rum punch. We're celebrating.'

'There's one more thing,' Marco said. 'I'd be honoured if you'd come to Turin to spend Christmas with me for real. We'd be near your father—but also, I know someone who has missed your friendship for four years.'

'Bianca?' Claudia asked quietly. 'But doesn't she think terrible things about me?'

'No,' Marco said. 'Hard as it will be for you to believe me, I never poisoned her against you. I was still trying to protect her. She knew we'd been involved, and out of respect for my feelings she let your friendship drop. Being on the other side of the Atlantic helped that.'

'I've missed her too,' Claudia said. 'It would be really wonderful to rekindle our friendship.'

A sudden joyful smile lit up Marco's face and he sprang to his feet, carrying Claudia with him in his enthusiasm.

'I love you so much!' he exclaimed, hugging her so energetically that her feet lifted off the floor.

Claudia laughed and clung happily to him, gasping with delight as he suddenly lifted her higher and spun her round and round, laughing with her in his happiness.

At last they came to rest next to the Christmas tree, and Claudia found herself looking with delight at the decorations—the branches were adorned with gorgeous glazed ceramic shapes and the cutest Christmas motifs and figures, made entirely from whole nutmegs, cinnamon sticks and other spices she didn't immediately recognise.

'They're all crafted locally,' Marco said.

'It's beautiful,' Claudia breathed, leaning close to the tree. 'And it smells like Christmas too. I love the scent of spices.'

'This is the Caribbean!' Marco exclaimed. 'A tropical paradise. I'll take you to places where the air is saturated with spice and every breath fills your lungs with the natural perfumes of exotic flowers.'

'That sounds amazing,' Claudia said, hugging him close once more. 'But I don't need to go anywhere to feel like that. Just being with you makes me feel like I'm in paradise.'

He hugged her back, wrapping his strong powerful arms around her in a way that made her forget everything but how wonderful it was to be held by him. Eventually they sank back down on to the sofa and he brought her a glass of rum punch.

She sipped the potent brew, unable to take her eyes off Marco's face, hardly able to believe how happy she felt. The beautiful glow of love filled her and the fiery heat of passion was starting to flow through her veins as she looked deep into his sultry eyes.

She lifted her hand and brushed her fingers through his black hair.

It was still stiff with salt from his swim the previous day and she realised he'd been too distraught to think about washing it.

'You need to shower and shave,' she said, smoothing her hand against his stubbled jaw line.

'Come with me,' he said. 'I need you with me.'

She knew he was talking about more than the shower. He needed her for the rest of their lives.

'Always,' she said. 'I'll love you always. And I'll be with you for ever.'

MILLS & BOON

MODERN

On sale 2nd January 2009

INNOCENT MISTRESS, ROYAL WIFE
by Robyn Donald

Prince Rafiq de Couteveille of Moraze blames Alexa Considine
for his sister's death and is out for revenge. Lexie can't
understand why she's attracted the Prince's attention.
However, Rafiq is irresistible, and she soon finds
herself bedded by royalty…

TAKEN FOR REVENGE, BEDDED FOR PLEASURE
by India Grey

Gorgeous Olivier Moreau has only one reason for
seducing innocent Bella Lawrence. However, when cold
revenge becomes red-hot passion, Olivier finds he
has no intention of letting her go…

THE BILLIONAIRE BOSS'S INNOCENT BRIDE
by Lindsay Armstrong

Max Goodwin needs a glamorous secretary – fast – and when
dowdy employee Alexandra Hill transforms into Cinderella, Max's
thoughts turn decidedly personal! However, Alex refuses to be
a mistress to anyone and Max will never take a wife…

THE BILLIONAIRE'S DEFIANT WIFE
by Amanda Browning

Prim and proper Aimi Carteret has put her tragic past
behind her. Now wealthy businessman Jonah Berkeley will
stop at nothing to breach her defences and get the feisty
woman he knows is underneath out and into his bed!

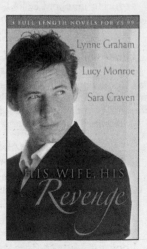

Celebrate 100 years of pure reading pleasure with Mills & Boon®

To mark our centenary, each month we're publishing a special 100th Birthday Edition. These celebratory editions are packed with extra features and include a FREE bonus story.

Plus, you have the chance to enter a fabulous monthly prize draw. See 100th Birthday Edition books for details.

Now that's worth celebrating!

September 2008

Crazy about her Spanish Boss by Rebecca Winters
Includes FREE bonus story
Rafael's Convenient Proposal

November 2008

The Rancher's Christmas Baby
by Cathy Gillen Thacker
Includes FREE bonus story *Baby's First Christmas*

December 2008

One Magical Christmas by Carol Marinelli
Includes FREE bonus story *Emergency at Bayside*

Look for Mills & Boon® 100th Birthday Editions at your favourite bookseller or visit
www.millsandboon.co.uk

FREE!

4 Books
and a surprise gift!

We would like to take this opportunity to thank you for reading this Mills & Boon® book by offering you the chance to take FOUR more specially selected titles from the Modern™ series absolutely FREE! We're also making this offer to introduce you to the benefits of the Mills & Boon® Book Club™—

- ★ **FREE home delivery**
- ★ **FREE gifts and competitions**
- ★ **FREE monthly Newsletter**
- ★ **Exclusive Mills & Boon Book Club offers**
- ★ **Books available before they're in the shops**

Accepting these FREE books and gift places you under no obligation to buy, you may cancel at any time, even after receiving your free shipment. Simply complete your details below and return the entire page to the address below. You don't even need a stamp!

YES! Please send me 4 free Modern books and a surprise gift. I understand that unless you hear from me, I will receive 6 superb new titles every month for just £2.99 each, postage and packing free. I am under no obligation to purchase any books and may cancel my subscription at any time. The free books and gift will be mine to keep in any case.

P8ZEF

Ms/Mrs/Miss/Mr ....Initials ....

Surname ....

Address.. **BLOCK CAPITALS PLEASE**

....

....Postcode ....

Send this whole page to:
UK: FREEPOST CN81, Croydon, CR9 3WZ